THE AFTER HOUSE

D0048352

Michael Phillip Cash

ISBN: 1500600369
ISBN 13: 9781500600365

Dedicated to my dad

Who got the ball rolling.

af·ter·house – *noun*- \\'af-tər-ˌhaus\\
    1.   the deckhouse nearest the stern of a ship

Prologue

Off the coast of Puerto Rico, 1840

Captain Eli Gaspar looked at his crew rowing rapidly toward the great sperm whale in the distance, the balmy air weighted with humidity. They had shipped out of Puerto Rico yesterday morning after restocking. They found a pod of whales and took a female and two calves. After a halfhearted chase, they towed them back and attached the carcasses to the ship. The heads were severed, and so began the arduous job of processing the beasts. Blanket pieces of the whales' skin were stripped off like the peel from an orange, lowered into the blubber room, and cut into small pieces.

Fires under large cauldrons worked for days, breaking down the fats into liquid. The rancid smell of burning blubber filled the ship. It permeated the men's clothing and the bedding. Their skin was black with grime. After being boiled, the oil was stored in casks until the men could head home to sell their bounty.

Eli was journeying home after thirteen months at sea. He had missed the birth of his son, little Charlotte was turning eight, and his father-in-law had broken his wife's heart by dying suddenly. Sarah's letter had caught up with him in the Canary Islands. She begged for him to hurry home. Money was tight, her father's estate tied up, and she needed him. You would think an attorney would have taken better care of his only child, but what was it they said about the shoemaker's children? They were the ones left barefoot. He knew Sarah was bereft. She needed him. She wasn't good with finances—hell, she wasn't good with decisions. She had her father for that, and now he was gone.

Eli couldn't imagine what he was going to find when he got home. The sooner he got there, the better. He wrote back but wasn't sure if he would return before his letter arrived. The mail at sea was, at best, unreliable.

It was a good trip. They had taken twenty-two whales. He was upset with the crew for killing the calves, but the first one had gotten in the way when they tried to harpoon the mother. The second one was clearly sick, based on what they discovered after cutting it open. They left that one for the ever-present sharks that circled the ship, made quick work of the mother and the other calf, then pushed north toward home.

Today the bull appeared out of nowhere, the large knobs of its backbone causing Eli's lookouts to scream, "She blows," as the sun sank into the silver-dappled water. It was huge. Eli gripped the rail. He had never seen anything as big as this one. It had to be over eighty feet long—almost as big as the bark he sailed. He watched in awe as the S-shaped blowhole blew a geyser toward the darkening heavens. It was late, the sun just about to dip into the horizon, but this was too great a prize to ignore. He tasted rain in the air and knew a storm was brewing. He hoped they'd capture the whale long before the expected squall reached them. The men jumped rapidly into the two whaleboats, seven in each, starting the chase that could last upward of twenty-four hours.

"They're a well-oiled crew," Eli thought proudly. They had drilled for days in the beginning of the trip, learning each other's quirks, making their response instantaneous when prey showed up.

The boats flew over the white-tipped waves, the air thickening with moisture, the storm moving their way with the same speed as Eli's seasoned rowers. The sea grew choppy, and the great whale disappeared under the surface. The lookout's frenzied movements with small colored flags directed the rushing boats to its location. Time was running out. In the east, the sky was turning the same deep blue as his wife's eyes. The first bright pinpoints of the stars lit the heavens above them. The west threatened rain. He glanced at the gathering storm clouds estimating how long they would have before the rain would compound their work.

"Row, you bastards. Give it to him!" Eli shouted the command to strike, his face burning from the wind.

The whale leaped up, mocking them with his fluke, arcing over the water to land in a huge splash. "Get him! Get him!" Eli ordered his first mate, pounding his fist with each word. He rolled onto the balls of his feet, leaning forward, caught in the thrill of the capture, a smile on his face.

The crew picked up speed, rowing efficiently, surrounding the animal. Moses, his first mate, stood majestically in the longboat, bracing his leg in the clumsy cleat to throw his iron. Time ceased then. The air was turgid, and everything moved in slow motion. Eli wished he could capture the moment somehow.

His burnished skin glistening with sweat, Moses raised the long rod majestically, aiming the harpoon. Moses was six foot five, ebony, with muscles honed from his years as a slave. He was a free man now, and Eli's first mate. Eli trusted him with his life. The sun was at half-mast, bathing the sparkling waves with red and gold. The two longboats and the crew were primed for the kill.

Eli heard the harpoon hit with a meaty thud. A cheer of satisfaction erupted in the boat, letting him know Moses had struck true. The big man glanced back, a smile splitting his dark face. Eli grinned back with shared satisfaction. A second boat moved up from the south, the opposite direction, and Eli watched breathlessly as the greeny, one of the younger crew members, readied his arm to hurl a harpoon at the wounded whale. Eli could see the young man's arm quivering from the strain. They were breaking him in for harpooning. He had long, muscled arms, but lacked patience. He had missed the female on his last excursion, causing no end of ridicule by his mates.

"Got him!" Eli yelled, smiling proudly at the boy, who beamed back, his face triumphant with joy. It was a clean hit, right next to the other harpoon, the dual barbs sunk deep into the whale's wrinkled skin. Eli pumped his fist in the air with approval, sharing his delight with the lad. He would be getting more duties after this. But there was no time for that now. The leviathan thrashed its great head, his platter-sized eye wild.

"Stern, all! Stern for your lives!" the captain shouted, knowing Moses was crying out the same command on the longboats. He watched the giant's tail twist in the water, the resulting waves causing the boats to be knocked around like toys. Eli considered the whale's head, bobbing in the water. It was huge, more than half the size of the whole torso, and would yield mounds of spermaceti, the most profitable part of the whale for its use in candles. What a prize to end the trip. His holds would be weighted down with enough oil to pay his debts and stay home for a whole year. He could give Sarah what she craved—attention. He smiled with satisfaction. Perhaps now her tone with him would not be as sharp—as edged with disappointment. Her complaints dominated all the letters from home.

His reflection and the crew's celebration were cut short when the taut ropes from the harpoons spun from their coil, the friction causing a small plume of smoke.

"Careful...careful," he urged, bringing his watchful eyes and his attention back to the drama on the sea. He saw his men grab tight to the oars as the boat was lifted to skim the water.

"A Nantucket sleigh ride," little Henry Falcon yelled with admiration. Eli ruffled his cabin boy's head, laughing at his excitement. It never failed to thrill him too. "I wish you let me go with them!"

"I promised to keep you safe, lad," he said, sharing a smile at the feeling of the capture. "Next year will be soon enough." But he knew there'd be a next year only if Sarah let him leave. She went along with this life because her father was home to watch over her and the children. Now he was gone, and it might mean a future of being landlocked. She begged him to open a store so he could be home all the time. He was her husband, her protector. Time for adventures was over—that was her constant refrain. He'd had his fun, had sailed for close to eleven years, but now he was a family man and should be home to take care of them.

But Sarah was miles from him and the ship. He didn't have to think about that. Instead, he looked at the longboats racing across the waves, the men gripping the sides, their faces frozen in exhilaration. What he wouldn't give to be on that longboat, but he had made a promise to Sarah that he wouldn't take unnecessary chances. Married men don't risk their lives, she had told him all those months ago.

Henry reached into his pocket and took out a small whale tooth and a lead pencil.

Eli watched the boy stare at the scene and then look at the unfinished etching on the tooth. "You have to draw it on paper first, lad, then tap the holes into the ivory."

Henry held up the sloppily done scrimshaw. "It's not very good," the boy lamented.

"Rather fine, I'm thinking, for a first try. Rather fine. Should get better with time." The captain nodded at the artwork.

"Next trip, perhaps you can show me some more ways to do the drawings," Henry said.

"Yes," Eli answered sadly. "Perhaps." He knew his days of sailing were over, with his father-in-law's death. There would be no more trips for him.

He heard a raucous cheer from the longboats. The whale changed direction, sending the boats twirling, dipping, then righting themselves. Eli watched, caught up in the excitement with Henry. Again, he wished he were out on the sea, steering the whaleboat, actually participating in the chase. He missed the danger of the boat skipping over the waves in hot pursuit of its prey. Instead, they watched the boats skim the water, dragged by the tiring beast. They were nearing the end.

He turned to the boy, his voice stern. "Aren't you supposed to be lighting the fires with Barney?" He gestured to the men springing into action below them. The boy looked down to the lower decks to see the ship's cooper, blacksmith, stewards, and cooks all preparing the equipment for the next two days, when they would break down the whale. He sighed, pocketing the whale tooth and causing Eli to laugh. This was not the glamorous side of whaling.

"Can't I stay until the flurry?" Henry pleaded. The flurry was the final minutes when the whale was known to swim in a tight circle until its fin surfaced, indicating it was over. They both turned to see the whale change direction once more, the circles growing smaller. "It's our last before we head home. Please, Captain," he added with disappointment, his large brown eyes imploring. He wiped impatiently at the moisture on his face.

"Aye, it's in your blood too, Henry," the captain said. Without a word, Eli nodded his assent, watching the whale pick up with a burst of speed. "There's life in this big fellow yet." He patted his pockets, wishing he had taken his pipe.

The creature took off, leaving a bloody trail. The boats were pulled by the giant bull. The chase could last all night. Some did. They could be dragged in the whale's wake for hours until it tired, and its great heart gave up. The whale made a tight circle, swinging the longboats so that they flew above the waves, soaring four feet above the sea. They landed with tooth-jarring violence. The whale paused, as if getting its bearings, then turned into the longboats.

"What's he up to?" Eli asked no one in particular, his hands gripping the rails.

"It's lobtailing!" Henry screamed in horror, his dark brown eyes wide, as the huge tail reached above the waterline. The beast hit the churning sea with its fluke, creating a sound like a cannon.

Eli heard wood splinter and watched with disbelief as the first boat disintegrated, men flying as if an explosive had torn into them. The whale leaped out of the water, his long razor of a jaw tangled in the lines. It gnawed on the thick ropes. He heard shouts as the men in the remaining boat tried to regroup, looking for survivors. The loud cries turned into screams as the whale arced, pulling the lines tight to dive deep. Eli gasped as the other boat disappeared under the waves, only to resurface seconds later, empty of men. The tail appeared again, flapping the water, crushing a lone seaman struggling to grab an oar.

"What's happening?" he yelled to the two men watching from the masts. "Launch boat three!" he called out to begin a rescue.

The lookout screamed, his eyes wild with horror. "It's heading for us!" He scrambled down the tall mast, his feet barely touching the pole. Eli ran across the slippery deck, watching the giant head part the waves to barrel toward them. This couldn't be happening. He was almost finished with his journey. This was the last whale before they headed for home. He had played it safe, just as his wife had asked.

The water turned wretchedly violent, the sky was black as pitch, opening up with a deluge and turning the horizon into a sodden mess. Sheets of water dropped from the heavens, obscuring the ocean.

He sprinted toward the wheel, his feet sliding. He fell heavily on his knee. It cracked in time with thunder, and white spots danced before Eli's eyes. He pounded the deck with his fist in frustration. Cursing at the pain, he pushed himself to his feet and threw himself at the wheel, grabbing it from the old tar who was manning it.

He wrestled with it, trying to turn the ship, hearing his man scream, "It's going to ram us!"

"Brace yourselves! Douse the fires!" Eli yelled to the remaining crew. Wrapping both arms in the spokes of the wheel, he planted his feet firmly on the deck. She was strong, his ship, filled to the brim with whale oil— heavy, but solid on the water. Still, he had heard of a ship, a whaler, destroyed by another whale somewhere in the Pacific recently. He didn't believe it possible, but he couldn't deny the story.

He saw Henry huddled in the corner, his small form shivering. His eyes were rounded with fear, his shoulders hunched. Eli was supposed to protect him. It was his job. He had given his word that he'd keep him from harm. This was not supposed to happen. He had promised the boy's mother a safe journey. He had promised Sarah his own safe return as well.

"Get to the afterhouse!" he yelled to the boy over the driving rain. "Go to the afterhouse! You'll be safe there!"

Henry stared at him, rigid with fear. The afterhouse was a small structure on one of the lower decks where men went to escape the elements, to stay dry. He looked at the captain, tears making tracks down his chubby cheeks. Eli's heart twisted in his chest. He had no time for this.

"Get below!" he bellowed. The boy stood frozen, looking small. He was too young to die. Eli pointed to the boxlike cabin below, his other arm straining to hold the spinning wheel. The boy responded as if shot. He gave a last anguished glance at Eli, then leaped, heading to the lower deck.

"Leave!" Eli shouted to the remaining sailors over the howl in the wind. "Batten yourself to anything! Go!"

The ship lurched as the angry whale slammed it. A great hole appeared in the side. Seawater came gushing in. Eli felt the ship tilt, his head connecting with the wheel. Dazed, he released the spokes, his fingers spasmodically trying to grab something, anything to hold onto. The ship tilted, and he slid off the deck, landing on the roof of the afterhouse with a loud thud. Water rushed around him, cold on his skin, making his teeth chatter. Blood ran from his brow into his eyes.

The ship was hit again, and great gouts of water splashed around him. Men's screams rent the air, muffled by the rain. His eyesight dimmed. The ship spun in a dizzying vortex. Eli gripped the wooden deck, pressing his face against its slick surface. He was going down, spinning in a circle. "I should have gone into the afterhouse," he thought dully. The afterhouse would have kept him safe.

His last thoughts were of his wife. He wondered how she was going to manage without him.

CHAPTER ONE

Cold Spring Harbor, winter 2014

The snow eddied and swirled down onto the pristine surface that glowed in the backyard. Remy Galway's thin shoulders shuddered as the cold seeped into her bones. She shifted from one foot to the other, regretting that they were bare. She briefly thought about climbing the narrow steps to get her ratty-looking slippers but felt too lazy. The wind whistled through the eaves, and she looked up, wondering if the three-hundred-year-old shingles would hold. "Well, they really aren't all three hundred years old," she thought. The landlord had replaced most of them when she'd rented the house the previous fall.

Her father had offered to buy the place. He had insisted. He wanted her safe and happy. She absolutely refused. She had taken enough from him and her mother and was determined to stand on her own two feet, the way Dad had done it himself. He was a big bear of a man, with wind-whipped cheeks and a full head of white hair. Her parents were comfortable, both retired, with healthy pensions and a roster of activities that kept them busy.

She was an only child, born to them late in life, the apple of their eye. Though there was a big age difference—her mom was well past forty, her father approaching fifty when she was born—they maintained a wonderful relationship. Growing up, they gave her everything they could, exposing her to ballet, yoga, the arts, white water rafting, and traveling the world. Her parents were much older than most of the other parents, and as a result, she didn't develop many friendships. She was a lonely child, dependent on them for company. They filled her life with pleasant memories, and for the most part, she had a picture-perfect childhood.

Remy enjoyed their company, her father's gentle humor, and her mother's insightful wit. She was closer to them than many of her contemporaries were to their parents, and she remembered her dismay when they didn't appreciate the man she chose to marry. It was nothing they could put their finger on, they told her, just a feeling. "Couldn't you wait a bit, and get to know him better?" her mother had asked.

Remy met Scott in Cancun, her last spring break of college, and fell head over heels for his vibrant personality. He was daring and funny, filled with great ideas for an exciting future. Her quiet and retiring nature was opposite to his freewheeling personality. Weekends were filled with parties and road trips—thrilling adventures for a sheltered girl. She was part of a couple, and Remy loved it.

Fresh out of college, they moved in together, searching for a business they could build from the ground up. Scott hated the idea of traditional jobs. They found an inexpensive food franchise. It was the newest trend—a lunch bistro. It was promoted as a sure thing, and Scott insisted it was perfect for them. It was not your average deli but a gourmet sandwich shop and very French. They studied up on the product and spent a week at the headquarters in South Carolina, learning every aspect of the business. They borrowed from her father, pouring their hearts and souls into the budding business. It was hard work, with long hours, and they made plenty of costly errors. They were smart and learned from those mistakes.

The shop did moderately well. They had chosen to rent space in a tiny strip mall that catered to an office complex situated behind them. Scott pounded the pavement, dropping off menus, shaking hands, giving out samples that built them a solid foundation of steady customers. Money got easier, but instead of repaying her father, Scott talked him into putting in more money for two additional sandwich shops. He made inquiries into buying an old food truck for a fleet that would bring their brand to all parts of the island. Scott worked all kinds of hours and stayed out for meetings with new investors.It was after they opened the third shop that Remy discovered she was pregnant. Her parents gave them a quiet wedding on the lawn of the house they'd built twenty-five years earlier overlooking the sound in Eastern Long Island. They didn't like Scott, she knew. They thought she was making a terrible mistake.

The night before her wedding, her dad spoke to her in her old bedroom. He sat on the bed, his face grim, his hands resting over hers. "It's only money," he said. "Remy, if you have the slightest doubt, we can call it off—no problem."

Remy shook her head. "He's fun, Dad. He makes me stretch myself, think outside the box."

Her father had an answer for everything. Brian paced the room. "You are so creative, bubbly. Any guy would be lucky to be with you. I can't put my finger on it, Rem. I just don't like the guy." Her father sat beside her, taking her small hands in his own. "Can't you see what a catch you are? Don't throw yourself away on someone who doesn't deserve you."

Finally, she whispered, "But I love him. I really do, Daddy."

Her father sighed sadly, got up the next morning, put on his best blue suit, and escorted her down the flower-strewn paper aisle on the lawn. Olivia came seven and a half months later, bringing great joy to Remy's aging parents. She admitted her father had tried with Scott but found him immature, and they had nothing in common. At first, she blamed the generational differences, but time and Scott's temper proved her parents right.

Things changed after Olivia's birth. Scott started staying out later and later for meetings with people that seemed not to yield anything. The food truck idea sizzled out. Scott was inconsolable. He blamed Remy for slowing down, not taking on enough responsibility in the restaurants, not working to her full capacity. She tried, but between the baby, her housework, and running from shop to shop, she was exhausted. It was hard. She forgot to order cold cuts. The house never was clean enough. He wanted her to drop Olivia at child care more often and for longer hours. They disagreed on parenting styles. Their time together became argumentative and filled with friction. Forget about the romantic part; who had time for that? She worked herself sick, getting a stomach flu that nearly killed her. Scott didn't even come home to help.

It seemed like Scott never got tired. His energy irritated Remy. He found fault with everything she did, and even minor tasks started becoming an issue. A cold war developed in their home. While Scott was attentive to Olivia, Remy felt ignored, abandoned. Revenue slowed down inexplicably. Scott stopped paying back the loan to her parents, as well as the mortgage on the ranch they had bought with their wedding money. Remy didn't even know they were in foreclosure until well after she found out Scott had been lying to her about more than their finances. It started with calls, hang-ups, followed by stores calling to confirm purchases she had never made. Mail with another woman's name on it arrived at her home. Once the lights were turned off, she knew they were sliding into deep trouble.

Scott refused to admit anything was wrong. He came home long after she went to sleep, leaving so early that she only knew he'd been there by the indent in his pillow. With dawning horror, she sat with the detective her father had hired, looking at pictures of Scott with another woman and a baby boy. There were pictures of them at the bank, the mall, out to eat. It seemed he had plenty of time and patience for the slender blonde he chose to be with. Remy's face reddened with shame. There were pictures of him at their sandwich shops holding the girl's hand and carrying his son in an infant seat. Remy lowered her head into her arms, too shocked to cry. In the stores! That meant even the employees who worked for them knew what was going on. She wanted to curl up and die.

"I debated telling you," her father told her, his amber eyes sad. Her parents flanked her in her tiny kitchen. The light hurt her eyes. "This is serious." Brian held her hand after the private investigator left. "He's going to drain you dry, honey. You have a child, you can't let him ruin your life."

"He just did," Remy answered tearfully.

Her mother made tea, the cure-all, and urged her to return home with them. They would help her in any way they could. She needed to regroup, her parents insisted.

"Do you think I should talk to him?"

"What?" Brian stood impatiently. "For what? How much are you going to take?"

"Brian, please," her mother said. "This is not the time. Remy, is that what you really want to do? Do you think you can salvage your relationship? Do you really want to, honey?" Her mother took her face, holding her cheeks as though she were a precious treasure. "Can you forgive what he's done?"

"We have a child," she said miserably. "He's not all to blame. I checked out too."

"Checked out!" Brian repeated with outrage. "Dogs have puppies too. Anyone can be a father, even an animal."

"Dad!" Remy said at the same time her mother called out, "Brian."

"He's a good father," Remy said.

"But a bad husband. Look, Remy, ultimately it's your decision. I...I never expected this to happen to you."

Remy hung her head.

"Kiddo, it's not your fault." He looked down at her, his face mirroring her anguish.

"Maybe it is."

"Remy, stop doing this to yourself. Think of Olivia."

So she did what she thought she should, confronting Scott when he returned later that night. He was tearful, filled with remorse, agreeing to do anything to save their marriage. They went for counseling. After the third session, Scott refused to go anymore.

His girlfriend and their newborn boy used up whatever funds they had saved from the bank. It finally ended with a bitter fight, Scott backhanding her when she demanded to know why he wouldn't return to the therapist. She left him that night, wondering how many times a heart could break. She took her daughter with her and moved into a motel for a week. She never told her daughter where her black eye came from, and she refused to allow her parents to discuss Scott in front of the child.

Olivia was bereft without Scott. He had the same magical effect on her child as he did on Remy in the beginning. Scott was a charmer and knew exactly how to make Olivia feel he was the victim in their breakup. Remy picked her battles, but she fought fair. She was devastated when the bistros closed within the month but was honest enough to admit that she was happy not to have to deal with Scott in a professional atmosphere.

Tail between her legs, she ran home to her parents, who facilitated the divorce. Remy found her yoga certification buried in the back of her old closet and took a job at the local gym. She was a good teacher, her style well regarded. Her classes were always filled. She began arranging private classes with many of the clients and supplemented her income. She was in great demand; her gentle instruction yielded results, and soon she was juggling a full schedule. Though her parents welcomed her, let her use their paneled basement for private sessions, she knew it was an imposition. She hated being dependent on them, like a child. She wanted her own place, needed a bit of freedom from their hovering.

She took on odd jobs, saving every penny she could. After having her own household, it was hard to move back in with the folks. She knew too, even though they never complained, that it wasn't fair to them either. She waitressed at night while she built up the small private yoga business, selling everything she had from her life with Scott on eBay. She rented space for a studio on Main Street. It was a large room in the lower level of a faded pastel building, nestled right in the center of Cold Spring Harbor. A hairdresser had the upstairs rental. Remy's space had a bathroom, complete with a changing area, and she was able to book teacher trainings that plumped up her bank account. Three local schools asked her to instruct the gym teachers. This led to business with more and more schools. Her dad hung up blinds, and her mom helped her paint the room a pale green. It wasn't long before she had put together funds to rent a three-hundred-year-old house in the small town, just blocks away from the studio. Olivia could walk to school. It was perfect.

Twelve Fourteen Spring Street was a tiny, white cottage with a handful of cozy rooms. The low, smoky ceiling gave her a feeling of security. Her dad told her she was three ways a fool for renting such an old place, but he did admit it was solid as the bedrock it was built on. Perched on a small hill behind Main Street, the house looked out over Eagle's Bay. A ribbon of a road separated the lawn from the calm water, and an ancient rose garden in the rear had been laid out the same way for three centuries. Remy knew it was filled with sixteen types of roses and couldn't wait to see them bloom.

She had a small kitchen with a giant fireplace on one wall and a huge Kasten, an original faded blue wooden Dutch cupboard, built into a spot against the wall. Her breakfast table was a refurbished antique door, the base a late-nineteenth-century sewing machine. Olivia always stretched her short feet to pump the pedal. Remy matched it with modern chairs, giving the room an eclectic look. She had collected copper pots at various yard sales, hanging them around the surround of the fireplace. The landlord, the nephew of the original owner, had replaced the appliances, and the room sported new stainless steel, which sparkled between the smoldering dark colors.

The last occupant had added a laundry room. He was a pretty famous artist who had lived in the house for over five decades. When senility set in, the nephew put him in assisted living and rented the cottage to her. She had painted and done some updating, but she was still waiting for an alarm system, phone, and cable to be put it. The old artist never even had a television set. The last two weeks had been challenging, with spotty cell phone service and no Internet.

She loved the small parlor, with its wide, planked floors and permanent smell of woodsmoke. An interesting mural covered an entire wall—a seascape with a whaler who was known to have shipped out of the local harbor. Not exactly her taste, but it was a condition of her rental that she not remove it. She wouldn't dream of it, especially because of Olivia's fascination with the bearded sea captain bleakly watching his ragtag crew manning a whaleboat.

Captain Eli, as he was called, stood on the top deck as sailors chased a great sperm whale, their longboat being pulled through the foamy waves. He gazed intently, his face giving the impression of unhappiness, while the crew seemed oblivious to it all. It did take some getting used to, but it was a piece of Americana, and Remy respected that. They also had a tiny study where they hung a television in anticipation of the cable service being activated.

The study was attached to a formal dining room she used for practicing yoga. Upstairs were two bedrooms—one for her and one for Olivia—and a black-and-white bathroom that begged for a renovation. Once the studio paid a profit, that would be her first project. Well, after she purchased it. She was determined to save up enough for a down payment. The home had been built in the early 1700s in the whaling town of Cold Spring Harbor. She knew that fact from the plaque nailed next to the front door under the address. Oddly enough, the house originally belonged to a whaling captain and his family. Perhaps the artist did his mural as an homage to them. However, now the snug place was hers and Olivia's, and nobody was going to tell her what to do anymore. Not ever.

The icy bay was quiet, but she could see the white-tipped waves curl against the rocky beach. Cupping her hands around her warm mug, she wandered out of the kitchen to sit in one of the winged chairs she kept before the fireplace in the small parlor. She felt her feet glide over the cool polished wood and then find relief as they warmed on the area rug that filled the center of the room. It was a Chinese rug she had appropriated from her parents' house. A bright emerald green, its border was filled with cream and light rose flowers. It had been rolled up in the attic, a leftover from Aunt Ruth's house, and was out of style. "But beggars can't be choosers," she thought with a sniff.

Olivia was not crazy about the house. They made a big deal about giving it a more feminine feel, but her daughter was unconvinced. Remy gave Olivia her first house key, attached to a fuzzy ball of pink fur, so she could get in all by herself. Olivia responded by announcing that she didn't even want to be in the house, much less have a key. She kept silently poking around the nooks and crannies, her great whiskey-brown eyes wide in her pale face.

"What are you looking for?" Remy asked her.

"I don't know, but when I find it, I'll tell you," Olivia said in her serious little voice. "I feel all goose bumpy here." She rubbed her hands together. "Mommy, do you think someone is watching us?"

"Don't be silly, Livie," Remy said with a chuckle. Still, there were times she felt as though she were not alone in the house. They joked about finding ghosts and ghouls, made a great game of it, but Remy had to admit that all that talk made her slightly uneasy. "Big baby," she would think when she caught herself entertaining such ideas. They blasted music, and Britney, Christina, Katie, and Lorde filled the old cottage with loud tempos to chase away the sullenness.

Still, Olivia seemed happy enough this weekend to leave her and spend the night at Scott's with his bimbo. It smarted, but Remy was determined not to ruin it for her child. No matter how immoral Scott was, Olivia deserved to have a relationship with her dad. A girl needed a father, and while he treated Remy cavalierly, at heart he was a good dad to Olivia. Remy resented his new family, but Olivia seemed OK about it. Her daughter's acceptance troubled her just a tiny bit, but she didn't want to rock the girl's boat any more than she had to. She had to carve out a new life, and she refused to let the bitterness of the divorce color it. Lots of kids lived like this. Scott would drop her off at school tomorrow, and Remy would have her until Wednesday. Though she didn't like it, it was her new reality.

She curled up on the saggy seat of the chair, the small fire she built earlier warming her cold cheeks. It crackled and hissed, spitting sparks that unnerved her. She jumped every time the wood popped from the intensity of the flames. Remy reached down to where she'd placed a new bottle of scotch. Holding it up, she gazed at the rich liquid. It was the same color as both her eyes and Olivia's. "God, I miss my daughter," she thought with a heartfelt sigh. The silence screamed at her, and she thought of fifty things to do but somehow couldn't muster up the energy to start anything. She had boxes to unpack, curtains to hang, drawers to line, but her hands felt heavy, her chest tight with the pain of being alone. Oh, she had her parents, but she was ashamed to admit she missed Scott.

She couldn't believe that after all he'd done to her, she could still feel the loss of him, but she did, and it made her angry. He was a shit, a total shit, yet when she thought of him, she had to remind herself of the pain she felt when he deceived her. For God's sake, he had punched her. Still, she wondered what part of it was her fault. Did some of the responsibility belong to her? What if they didn't have the money pressures? Maybe she could have worked harder.

"What if we'd waited to have a child?" she wondered. Olivia was the best thing that ever happened to her. Ever. Period. In the end, her parents were right about Scott. Her innocent and love-struck eyes failed to see the monster she tangled with. She touched the spot on her face where he had bruised her over a year ago. It didn't hurt anymore, of course. It had healed, as it was supposed to, but her heart never had. Scott was wrong, she reminded herself. She rolled her head against the chair, feeling oppressed. Her face grew hot, her lips quivered, but she fought the tears. This was just the beginning. She had to adjust. The empty future yawned ahead of her, frightening her. She had picked that loser. She missed every sign, was blind to his faults, trusted her schoolgirlish heart to tell her she was in love. Remy shivered, knowing she was afraid to trust her judgment about men anymore. She realized she'd better get used to being alone.

Loneliness was a state of mind, she reasoned. If she chose not to focus on it, maybe it would disappear, like the fog rolling over the waves. Her eyes returned to the empty room, the shadows painting the walls. Olivia's discarded coloring book lie on a footrest. Her crayons were scattered about the end table. Remy knew she should put it all away, but she just didn't want to. The house seemed devoid of life, missing the childlike joy Olivia brought to any room. "This sucks," Remy thought as she pouted. She placed her mug in the fold of her lap, unscrewed the top on the bottle, and shakily poured…a what? A tot? A dram? Whatever—a gulp of scotch into her half-finished tea. Remy took a healthy swig of the tea. The liquor burned behind her nose and traveled down to the pit of her empty stomach. She shook herself with a grimace. She wondered what people could possibly like in the stuff. It tasted like iodine. Not that she knew what iodine tasted like, but she figured it probably tasted like scotch.

Not one to waste things, she took another sip, this one more tentatively. She found it not as distasteful, instead experiencing a delightful lassitude that relaxed her brittle muscles. Another sip made her feel more comfortable with the brew, and by the time she was sucking on the dregs of her cup, nothing was bothering her anymore—not the weather, not her ex, not being alone, and certainly not the weird shifting of the shadows in the hallway of her little house. "Nope," she thought, holding the empty cup against her cheek. "Nothing's going to bother me tonight."

She ran her fingers through her chestnut hair, considering the feathered ends. She had straight brows complemented by direct amber eyes. A delicate jaw with a slightly pointed chin gave her a pixie look. She was petite but strong. Yoga gave her a firm body, and though she looked slight, she was toned and flexible. The firelight played with her creamy skin, and her small, straight nose flared each time Scott entered her thoughts. A light dusting of freckles saved her face from any seriousness.

The house creaked eerily. Remy reached over to the other chair to grab the afghan her mother had made her when Remy had left for college. It was blue and white, her school colors, completely out of place with the muted grays and greens of her quiet little cottage. She wrapped it around her cold feet, and the familiar weight of the heavy wool made her feel safe and secure. She could have slept at her parents'. They told her often enough, but Remy knew she had to stick this night out alone. She had to prove to herself she could be solo. Time to put on the big-girl panties.

Every Wednesday and alternate weekends, Olivia was going to sleep at the home of Scott and his girlfriend, Prunella, or whatever her name was. Remy refused to go back to her old frilly bedroom in Sayville, like she had in the beginning of her separation. She was divorced now. Three weeks short of a year. A divorced woman, single, and she better get used to it. Never in a million years did she think it would end up like this.

Her toe poked a hole through the old knitted blanket. It was getting shabby. They'd both seen better days. Remy gazed at the dying embers of the fire. Here and there, a small flare would paint the walls orange as it bathed her face with warmth. She thought she should go up to the tiny bedroom at the top of the steep steps, but she couldn't gather up the motivation. The snow turned to rain, which pattered against the leaded glass. Pulling her knees close to her chest, she buried her chin against the soft wool. A small tear rolled down her peach-tinted skin to land with a plop. She stared at the mural, her eyes always finding the captain, his face stark with longing. Why did she think he looked angry when they moved in? How had she missed the sadness in his face?

She felt an emptiness. Loneliness overwhelmed her. She looked at the deep-set dark eyes following the crew and wondered if their bleakness mirrored her own. Another crystal tear dampened her cheek, and soon they streamed down her face, gilding her skin in the firelight.

* * *

Eli couldn't believe it. She was a watering pot. He toyed with a candy dish, debating where to throw it, but her mood stopped him. He watched the tears flow silently down her cheeks and reconsidered what he was planning. She cried prettily, he admitted to himself. He sat on his haunches, directly beside her, watching the slow, silent progress of her tears. This woman knew grief. It tugged directly at his heart, making a bridge of understanding.

She was so quiet, he had to peer closely to see the hurt in her face. It was as though she didn't want to inflict her pain on anyone else. Oh, he had watched her interact with others. She was brave. He'd give her that.

He reached out to touch her smooth cheek but pulled his hand back guiltily. A memory intruded, another tear-streaked face. Long, gulping sobs filled his ears. The cries grew louder. He saw images of a woman with patchy red blotches ruining the soft lines of her skin. Screams filled his head, and he covered his ears, trying to silence the noise. Screwing his eyes shut, he blocked the sight, but the sound of the elusive woman's distress came from inside his head.

The cries grew distant, then they faded, and Eli shuddered in relief. He had been having a rough few weeks. The woman and her child moved in within a few days of Pat's departure. He hadn't interfered much; he watched them intently from the sidelines. They cleaned the old cottage with a vengeance, this pretty one with an older woman, probably her mother. An old salt helped out a lot. He was handy, and Eli admitted to himself that he liked the old guy.

There was nothing precisely wrong with what they were doing. Eli was known to run a tight ship, and the last few years, old Pat had neglected the place. It was nice to see the surfaces shining again, windows clean, floors polished. It was the kid that bothered him. A snippet of a girl, she followed him around. She considered the mural for hours, asking stupid questions. He'd settle in to watch them work and turn to find the little creep soundlessly sneaking up on him. More than once, he nearly fell off the mantle. She had an uncanny ability to zero in on his spot, then stare hard at him. He'd have to work on something—something good to teach the little miss to leave him alone.

He spied the discarded scotch bottle on the floor, his mouth watering. It had been so long, he thought, remembering the burn of liquor on the back of his throat. What he wouldn't give for a swallow. He eyed the female contemptuously. "Snap out of it, sailor," he wanted to shout. "Nothing like a little fright to put things into perspective," he thought grimly. "This ought to push her out of the doldrums."

He leaned down close to her ear and opened his mouth for a blast, when the gentle fragrance of lilacs drifted up, freezing him in his tracks. He cocked his head, letting the smell envelop him. Eli closed his eyes for a minute, holding the scent, letting it fill every part of his body. He floated lazily, feeling crisp sheets and the tender touch of a soft feminine body next to his. Tingling, he reached out for…for what? The memory disintegrated, leaving the ticking of the old schoolhouse clock and Remy's depression.

He squeezed his eyes shut, trying hard to bring it back, but it was gone—the feeling, the scent, and the aura of peace. Anger filled him. He looked down at the sad female and was furious at the impotence of trying to catch the chimera of a memory. He deflected his disappointment onto her. What could be so bad that she had to sit like this? The brat wasn't around. She had the night to herself and a twelve-year-old scotch right in front of her. Anger boiled inside him, and he felt himself swelling. He hovered over her head, seeing the shiny path of tears on her soft cheeks. It didn't seem right.

She sniffed loudly, then scrubbed her face with her sleeve. For a second, he conjured up an old memory of his cabin boy. What was his name? Henry. Henry Finch. No, no—Henry Falcon. He was supposed to do something for Henry and his mother. He tried hard to find the memory but failed. All he saw was a faded image of the boy, the end near, silent tears running down the brave lad's face. Blood, so much blood, the decks were slick with it. Rain plastered the dark head, and his lips were caught in a frozen rictus of fear. What was happening to him? He was losing his edge. Cursing loudly, he kicked the bottle of scotch and flew up the chimney to sulk the rest of the night.

* * *

Glass rolled on the uneven floorboards, startling Remy from her thoughts. She sat up straight, her heart beating wildly in her chest as her nervous eyes scanned the darkened room. Reaching down, she righted the bottle. Her eyes searched the chamber, her fingers shaking with the uneasy feeling she was being watched. She looked at the twisting patterns on the wall, the play of light from the moon streaming in. There was no one there. No one at all. She must have tipped it.

She shivered uncontrollably. Goose bumps spread across her chest. Wrapping the blanket over her shoulders, she raced up the rickety stairs, darting into her bedroom and closing the door firmly behind her.

CHAPTER TWO

Eli hung on the eaves of the house like an angry bat, stewing over the lost opportunity. It wouldn't take much, he knew. The woman was spooked, but in a way, so was he. He had to think. Memories like faded old pictures were intruding, making him uncomfortable, shaky, and insecure. This was no way to captain a ship. "Get your stuff together, old boy," he thought. "Concentrate on what you know." He summoned his logical side.

It wasn't that he had anything against the female, but he reasoned that everyone knew women on board brought bad joss—bad luck. He stood and began pacing back and forth over the phantom deck, feeling the salty spray splash his cheeks. His sea-crusted lashes scanned the dark horizon while he pondered his situation. The former inhabitant had recently died, leaving the house empty. They had shared the space for years, more than a half a century. Eli had a good relationship with the old man. Eli didn't bother him, and good old Pat Redmond happily returned the favor.

Pat was an artist whose marine paintings were prized among collectors. He was a loner—some said a little off, a bit strange—with only one nephew who visited at Christmastime. Eli liked talking to the old man. He spoke softly in his ear at night, describing vivid pictures of voyages he'd witnessed, helping the painter create beautiful and expensive art. Pat Redmond became known for his realistic portrayals of whalers and their crews. Now some of his paintings graced museum walls. Made him some big money. His fame brought him a lot of notice. Newspaper reporters wanted to write articles, but old Pat Redmond sent them all away. He wanted to be left alone in his little cottage. He was a familiar figure in the town, but nobody could figure out how he knew the minute details of the whaling trade. Since Pat was reclusive and quiet, the two of them found a way to coexist peacefully.

But the years passed, and the man aged. He became reckless, started telling people about Eli. In the beginning, his nephew found it amusing, but as time passed and stories became more involved, he worried about his uncle. The nephew hired a Jamaican woman to come every day. At first Eli observed her, shocked by her off-key singing. She was a large woman, her head covered by a colorful scarf. She walked the house intently, her eyes searching until they settled on him. She felt his presence.

He knew she saw him. She crossed herself frantically when he entered the room, her eyes widening, no matter how quiet he tried to be. He did try to be polite, nonintrusive, but she was definitely spooked by him. He could hear the hushed patois of her prayers. She banged pots and pans loudly when he flew above them. As if that would make a difference. He chuckled.

She placed salt in the corners and painted large stars with Pat's white paint—the water-based one, of course. Constantly sweeping the area with her broom, she generally disturbed any peace in the house. When she started sprinkling holy water around, as if he were the devil, he had just about had enough. Her presence made it impossible for him to talk to Pat. So he started doing things. Clearly he had no choice. She was interfering, making life intolerable onboard. That was the thing; women weren't supposed to be on the ship. Bad luck. Something terrible could happen.

He dropped the sugar bowl so that the white contents fanned out across the dining room floor in the shape of a whale. He knocked over a table or two, made the pictures on the walls all crooked, stole her shawl, slammed doors—the usual stuff. Nothing really horrific. He was, after all, still a gentleman. Just a little something to scare her off the property. He should have known what was going to happen, should have been better prepared, but Sarah always said he was a cloth head.

The woman came in the next day with a live chicken and sacrificed it in the kitchen. Its squawking scared the shit out of Eli. She waved the bloody carcass at him, the head bobbing, blood and chicken droppings splattering the floor.

He stood in frozen horror. He had to do something fast. Concentrating hard, he forced himself to materialize as she started plucking the chicken for Pat's soup. Delilah screamed shrilly and threw the damn chicken at him. Its carcass smacked against the wall loudly, startling old Pat into wailing like a banshee about flying dead poultry.

Well, that brought the neighbors, an effeminate lawyer and his husband, barreling into the small house brandishing golf clubs. Two men married to each other! They even wore rings. Eli was astonished. He rolled around the room laughing himself sick. The lawyer took in the bloody bird, Pat talking to the empty corner, and Delilah throwing water from a dark bottle at the shadows on the wall. The dandy passed out, knocking Pat right out of his chair. Well, Pat hit his head, and that was the end of that. He was placed in the nursing home lickety-split, where Eli knew he wouldn't last too long. Weeks later, he quietly died in his sleep.

Eli stayed with him, helping him cross, startled to see the young man Pat once was when he first purchased the old house. They visited a bit, spoke of times past, and then, somehow, Pat was gone. Eli wasn't sure where or how, but he'd bet boot nails to bobbins it had something to do with the two pale-faced, white-haired loobies he'd seen lurking around the place. He used his best material on them but received barely a nod. Cold as ice, they were, reminding him of the old sailor who found him after three days floating in a tangle of seaweed, deader than last week's fish. Had those same vacant-looking eyes. "Well," he thought. "Two can play that game." Every time he caught sight of the shiny material of their clothes, he shut down, making himself as blank as them.

Either way, he missed the artist. They ran a tight operation—no waste and everything was ship shape.

"Those were the days," he thought ruefully. Now not only did he have one female, but she brought along another. Beastly child. Eli shook his head. She followed him everywhere. A man couldn't think with the infantry on board. She was a quiet little thing, able to sneak up when he wasn't expecting anyone. It was wrong, all wrong. The whole thing got twisted up somehow. To top it off, they were changing things in the house. What was so bad that they had to fiddle with it? Everything had been fine for years and years. Pat liked it, the family before—the Hensons—were happy, and the couple before that, and so it went.

This, however, was a horse of a different color. They painted the bedrooms pink! There were flowers everywhere, fluffy pillows, ribbons—the house was fair to bursting with fripperies. Unnecessary furbelows, gimcracks, and don't get him started on the music, if that's what you wanted to call it. They irritated him. Whiny, interfering females cluttering up his home, filling it with nonsense, leaving him no peace. That's what Eli craved, peace, and now he had a decided lack of it. Someone was going to have to leave, and Eli knew he had nowhere special to go.

He entered the bedroom—pink like a pig's skin, cloying, sweet, not the least bit subtle—and gazed at the woman. She was on her side, her small hand curled under her cheek, the damp tracks of her tears visible. He lowered himself to her dressing table, looking at his reflection in the mirror over the messy surface. The image wavered, like simmering heat over sand, then settled into the familiar lines of his face. He was tall by nineteenth-century standards, with coal-black hair—dark as a raven wing, he recalled someone once saying. A close-shaved beard lined his lean cheeks, and his black eyes darted around the room. His aquiline nose, inherited from some noble, French ancestor, saved his face from being too beautiful. He touched the scar that bisected his dark brow, trying to remember just where he got it. The memory eluded him. The fleeting images flitted through his head but refused to settle.

He ran his nails across her comb and touched the delicate doily that covered the surface of her dresser. His calloused fingers snagged in the lace. He raised the corner and rubbed it between his fingers. Indistinct images teased his brain, and he tried hard to grasp them. They flickered like a dying flame, leaving only the remnant of charred ashes. He picked up a perfume bottle and lifted the glass stopper to inhale the scent. It tickled his nose, making his eyes tear. A woman's laugh echoed loudly in his head.

He caught sight of the white-haired ones with the dead-fish-looking skin observing him from above the window. Turning, he sneered at them, his teeth transforming into fangs, his eyes dripping blood.

He distinctly heard the male chuckle as he whispered, "Parlor tricks, Eli? Is that all you've got?" They were gone in a blink.

Eli spun, searching for them, ready to throw a fireball at their iridescent clothes, but couldn't find them. He replaced the cap of the perfume lid heavily. It teetered, then fell with the clink of glass, filling the room with the familiar smell.

The female sat up, her eyes reflecting light like a cat's. Eli's breath caught as the amber gaze searched the room. He hadn't noticed her eyes before. They lit up the night eerily.

"Baltic amber," he whispered. Her eyes were the color of Baltic amber. He had bought earbobs, for...for... whom?

* * *

"Who's there?" she demanded, holding the cover against her chest. Her breath came in short pants. "Scott?" she whispered. Reaching down, Remy grabbed a baseball bat she'd stashed under the box spring, then she carefully got out of the bed. Holding the bat defensively, she sniffed, smelling the overpowering odor of her perfume heavy in the night air. She walked toward the dressing table, shivering as she was encased in freezing air. Spinning, she looked at the window, squinting to make sure it was closed. She swung the bat into the nothingness before her, registering she was alone.

She lit a lamp on the dressing table and righted her spilt cologne. Her eyes scanned the top of the dresser, looking for a reason the perfume fell. She pulled several tissues from a box and sopped up the spilled liquid. Remy looked around the empty room, wondering why she was thinking of Baltic amber.

* * *

"You think he'll remember?" Marum asked from her perch under the roof.

Sten clicked his tongue impatiently. Vacation was over. They had been recalled earlier than he had hoped. "I'm not a mind reader," he said testily.

"That's not what they told me when they paired me with you." She looked at him sideways.

"Well," he conceded, "I am, but that's neither here nor there. I guess the universe feels Captain Eli has laid around here long enough and needs a gentle reminder."

"I hardly think Olivia's a gentle reminder." Marum smiled, her white teeth gleaming. "She's got more impact than the chicken." They both grinned.

"Oh, the chicken incident, that was priceless." Sten laughed. "Olivia's hardly subtle, but sometimes they need a little jolt."

Their iridescent clothes gleamed in the moonlight. Marum rubbed her back against the support beam of the house.

"Uncomfortable, are you?" Sten asked, his blue eyes concerned.

"Itches." Marum was grumpy.

"You'll get used to it." Sten stood, brushing off imaginary lint from his shiny pants.

Marum raised her pure, white brow. Her bright eyes were mischievous. "Here he comes," she said as they faded into the ether.

CHAPTER THREE

Remy came awake with a start, the sound of clinking glass alerting her that she was not alone. She reached over and grabbed the bat from the other side of the bed. She had slept with it next to her for the remainder of the night. The noise was coming from the kitchen, so she padded down the stairs, her back to the wall. Rounding the corner, she tiptoed into the kitchen and found her father washing the dishes in her sink.

"Dad!" She bounced into the room.

He turned, opening his arms to embrace her. He always made her feel tiny in his bearlike hug. He kissed her cheek roundly, then motioned to the table.

"I made you coffee," he said in a gruff voice. He tousled her hair. "Go get dressed, Remy. I'm making eggs."

"You don't have to, Dad. I'm not hungry."

"Get dressed, sailor." He peered closely at her. "This galley is a mess." He was an old navy man and had served in the Mediterranean in his twenties. "Hop to it!"

Remy raced for the steps, showering and dressing in record time. He set a plate before her, brimming with buttered eggs.

"I'm surprised at you, Rem. I don't expect to come in here and find a sink full of dirty dishes or a half-finished bottle of scotch."

"It fell, and some of it spilled." Remy shrugged, her mouth full of eggs. She refused to meet his eyes. "Where's Mom?"

"At some library thing in town. I dropped her off." He glanced at his watch. "I don't have much time. Do you want to come home? The nights when Olivia's with Scott will pass faster if you stayed with us."

Remy shook her head. "Thanks. I did OK. Olivia will be home later today. I have things to do at the studio." She reached over to cover his age-spotted hand with her own. "Thanks, Dad. It wasn't as hard as I thought."

Brian Tanner's faded amber eyes took in his daughter's pale face. "This isn't what I planned for you."

"Stop."

"You deserved better. I thought you might make a match of it with David," he said, referring to her first boyfriend.

"Dad, that was ages ago. High school stuff."

"I never liked Scott."

"I know, and I should have listened, but I didn't."

"The man has no honor," Brian said through gritted teeth.

"He's Olivia's dad." Remy laid her fist on the table. "We have a child between us, and I'll have to deal with him for the rest of my life."

"Not if I can help it," Brian growled.

"Dad, we'll find a way to work with each other."

"He hit you!" Brian stood to place the dirty dishes in the sink, his back rigid.

"I have a protective order. He can't come near me except to pick up Olivia. Please, Dad. I have to find my way in this thing. You have to stop being mad. Millions of women live like this."

"Not my daughter!"

Remy sighed and smiled. He loved her so, her dad. When she showed up on his doorstep with a black eye, both she and her mother had to restrain him from going after Scott.

"Yes, your daughter. But I am not a victim anymore. I left, and no one is going to bully me ever again." She stood and wrapped her arms around him, her nose squashed against the bulky fisherman's sweater he wore. She heard the reassuring thud of his heart and closed her eyes. The familiar smell of her father, and safety, enveloped her.

"Look, Dad, let's put it all behind us. It's time to move on."

He kissed the top of her head, then rested his chin there. "You know it wasn't you. You were a great wife."

Remy opened her mouth to reply, but the words caught in her throat. She wanted to believe that, but she accepted that some of the failure in the marriage may have rested with her as well. She just wasn't quite sure how. Something was just not right. She knew now that what she felt for Scott was enjoyment, affection, but not love. She understood love better since having Olivia. If Scott had really loved her, he couldn't have looked at her the way he did toward the end. She winced, the memories of Scott's red face screaming at her, blaming her, filling her head.

Her father shook her gently. "I mean it, Remy. Scott's an asshole."

"You won't get an argument from me about that." She smiled up at him.

"Let's go find Mom and have a snack in town before we head home. Oh, I forgot. Mom asked me to drop this off." Brian reached over and pulled out a framed needlepoint from a shopping bag he'd left by the back door. He smiled fondly as he looked at it. "She made it for you."

Remy admired it. "Oh, Olivia's going to love it."

They placed it on the kitchen table, then bundled up in layers to walk in the snow toward the library in town. The door closed behind them, muting their conversation.

Captain Eli waited for them to leave, then circled around to float over the picture.

* * *

The needlepoint rose off the table and fell with a crash onto the floor, the glass frame shattering. Eli kicked it against the wall, breaking the wooden frame. He stood above it, then jumped down, smashing it.

The sentinels observed calmly from their spot in the upper level.

"Do we interfere?" Marum asked as the broken needlepoint flew past them.

"You know the rules," Sten said softly. "He's really not doing anything too harmful."

"Captain Eli is having a moment," Marum said sarcastically.

"A temper tantrum, nothing more." Sten was bored. His laser-blue eyes watched dispassionately.

"This kind of behavior is getting him nowhere."

"Isn't that the problem, Marum? He's as stuck as we are right now. I can't watch. I'm going."

Eli wailed furiously, holding the tattered remains of the picture in his shaking hands.

"I don't believe this! Look what they're doing to my ship." He hissed with distaste. "Kittens!"

CHAPTER FOUR

J udith Tanner was attractive, with short gray hair cut in the same fashion since her twenties. She had a trim figure, with sparkling, blue eyes. She turned those orbs toward her daughter, smiling as Remy related her first night alone in the house. She neatly pleated the napkin. She was used to her hands always being busy. They were in a small shop on the main street, drinking tea with delightful lemon cakes. They sat by a picture-frame window, surrounded by shelves filled with lacy dolls and assorted accessories. There were tatted bags, flowered shawls, fingerless gloves—Judith was in heaven. She adored antiques, even if they were twenty-first-century reproductions.

Brian looked uncomfortable in the flimsy chair, his big frame filling the tiny seat. His thick fingers looked incongruous with the delicate porcelain tea set. Outside, traffic built up on the narrow street, the slush from last night's storm muffling the sound.

Judith couldn't wait to bring her granddaughter here. "When is Olivia coming home?" she asked.

Remy shrugged. "Not until this afternoon. Scott's dropping her off at school, and she has a playdate. He'll get her every Wednesday and then alternate weekends." She frowned. "I'll pick her up after five."

"A playdate." Judith brightened. "With whom?"

"One of her classmates. Her mother is a dance teacher, and her father is a realtor in the neighborhood. Nice people," Remy said wistfully, her gaze focused out the window.

Brian and Judith exchanged glances filled with silent communication. "Your old room is all prepared if you want it," Judith said. "You don't have to stay alone. Nobody will think less of you."

Remy smiled at them. She loved how her father knew what her mother was thinking before she even said it. She observed their shared looks, the ways their eyes caressed each other.

Once she asked her mom why she picked her father to marry.

Her mother had smiled cryptically and said, "Once you know, you just know."

Sometimes she felt like an intruder when she was with them, as if they belonged to a separate world all their own. She had expected the same relationship with Scott. Why didn't she get that knowing feeling with Scott? Remy shook off her feelings, then took a sip of her tea.

"Can't. I have a private at four."

"Oh, who?" Her mother raised a penciled eyebrow.

It aged her so, her makeup, but no matter how much Remy protested, she refused to update her style. It really didn't matter. She loved watching her father's expression when she caught him looking at her mother. The amber softened to a buttery glow. His love was palpable. It made her go all mushy inside every time she saw it. "Did Scott ever look at me like that," she wondered.

"Everything OK?" Her father's concerned gaze locked with hers.

"Yep." She sighed. "I'm fine. Molly booked a whole package. She's the woman who rented the cottage to me. She wants to give yoga a try."

"Go gentle with her," her father advised. "She'll bring you a lot of new clients."

"Yup. I'll take it slow. She knows everybody here."

Brian shook his head. "You should put up signs in all these stores." His sharp eyes scanned the room. "It's all, you know…"

"What, Dad?"

"You know, those yoga kind of people here."

Remy agreed with a contented smile. "I love it. It's like an artist's community."

Brian tapped his foot impatiently. "I don't think you're going to make enough to support—"

"It's lovely here," said his wife as she shot him a warning look. She patted her daughter's hand reassuringly. "It is like an artist's colony. I spoke with the curator of the museum."

"Museum?"

"The church has been bought by some kind of historical society. There's a very nice young man…" She took out a sheaf of papers from her purse. "Hugh." She read absently from the top paper. "He runs the museum, and he's very handsome—a little shy, but very good-looking."

Remy rolled her eyes. "Hugh who?" Remy asked, and then she laughed out loud. It was the first time she'd laughed in a long time, and she watched her parents enjoy it.

"Hugh Matthews. Tall, dark, and—"

"And I am so not interested. What does that have to do with artists?"

"Oh, the cottage—the one you're renting—was previously owned by an artist. Patrick Redmond. Look." She showed her a pamphlet. "He was famous for recreating oils of the whaling ships that sailed here. His paintings were somewhat of a mystery because of their accuracy. I mean, it was before the days of the Internet."

"I'm sure there was a way to get records," Brian said.

"It's the oddest thing." Her mother's face was alight with interest. "Hugh said—"

"Hugh?" her father asked. "How long ago did you meet him?"

"Just this morning. He's writing a book about Redmond. He's adorable, available, and he'd like to have coffee with you."

"With me?" Brain asked incredulously.

"No. Remy." She smiled encouragingly at her daughter.

Remy shook her head and whispered, "No. Told you…not interested. Not yet." Remy admitted to herself that she was gun-shy. "Dating," she thought with a shudder. She wanted to gag.

"Me either," Brian added with a nod. He didn't know if he wanted Remy with someone yet. She looked so small in her chair, so vulnerable.

Judith shook her head in exasperation. "Anyway, Hugh said the records were destroyed in a fire a hundred years ago. Recently they've been able to compile information with the help of the folks at Huntington Harbor. Patrick Redmond was a recluse, never left the town, yet he reproduced paintings that illustrated sailing techniques and the movements of the ships with precision. He's so bright."

"Patrick Redmond?" Remy asked, her mouth filled with a cranberry square.

"No, Hugh."

"Who?" Remy asked.

"Not who, Hugh." Judith drew out his name patiently.

"I'm sure there were letters or books," Brian said impatiently. "He lived here. He must have been a sailing man."

"Who, Hugh?" Remy asked, darting a puzzled look.

"No, Patrick Redmond." Judith shook her head. "That's the thing. Redmond was afraid of water and never went on the boats. There are no records of letters coming to him. You know the cottage had no phones, television, or Internet."

"That's the truth," Remy said after she took a sip of tea. "They're having a real difficult time finding ways to wire it up."

Brian raised his white brow in skepticism. "He should have given you a better price on the rent."

"Well, it is a small town," Judith retorted, ignoring their tangent.

Remy bit into another scone. "I read about something like that last week in a magazine at the dentist's. You know that movie *Ben Hur*, with Charlton Heston?"

"The one they play Easter time?" her mother asked as she pulled apart a turnover. She popped half in her mouth.

Remy really had to talk to her about that lip color. It was probably popular during the real Ben Hur's lifetime. "Yeah, well, it's based on a book written by some guy who never traveled to the Middle East, never studied anything about ancient history. He wrote a book that was incredibly historically accurate. He said he was directed by a greater power."

"Greater power!" Brian growled. "It's all bullshit as far as I'm concerned."

"What about Mozart or Einstein?" her mother said. "They say sometimes these people's genius comes from the unfinished lives of souls that lived before them." Judith's penciled brows rose until they were hidden by her bangs. Remy thought they looked better that way.

"Oh, come now, Judy!" Her father was ready to debate. "That's a crock, and you know it."

"I don't know, Brian. There are mysteries that beg to be solved. I watched a program on Bravo—"

"I don't want to hear about those housewives," Brian said.

"It was about people who communicate with the dead."

"TLC," Remy said.

"Tender loving care?" Judith asked.

"No, Mom, it was on TLC, the Learning Channel. I saw it too. One of the mediums is local."

"I think you're both loco," Brian said.

"I said local. Shhhh." Remy shushed her dad as she stood, her face alight as the door opened to admit a bundled-up customer.

"Hi!" she said to the full-sized woman with long, blond hair. She was bustling into the shop, pulling off colorful mittens to reveal long, cherry-red nails. "Molly!" She waved her over.

"Hi, Remy!" Molly rushed over, her eyes streaming, her nose as bright red as her polish. "Are you ready for me today?" she asked with excitement.

"Of course. Mom, Dad, this is Molly Caselle, my realtor."

"Molly Valenti now." Molly showed off a filigree wedding band.

"Congratulations. How long have you been married?" Judith asked.

"Six months. Oh, oh, Remy! We have to turn our session into a prenatal class." Molly could barely contain herself. She and Sal were expecting.

"That's wonderful, Molly." Remy hugged her. "Sit down. Can we get you something?"

"I don't have time. I have to bring back coffee for my associate." The waitress brought over a bag, advising her to be careful with the drinks inside. "See you at four," she trilled, heading out into the busy street.

"She's a little old to be pregnant," Brian said.

"Not much older than I was," Judith said. "Are you sure you'll be all right tonight?"

"Mom," Remy said with exasperation. "I was fine last night. Besides, Livie comes home today, remember?"

Brian wanted to ask why she needed the scotch if she was all right, but he chose to keep his mouth shut. She had to figure it all out. After all, they weren't going to be here forever.

CHAPTER FIVE

O livia skipped hand in hand with the new girl she'd met. She was on the way to Stella's house to spend the afternoon. She had spent the weekend at her father's, and he had dropped her off this morning at school. She really missed her mom, but Stella had invited her over, and she didn't want to disappoint her new friend. Stella was the nicest girl she'd met so far in the new school. They nodded to each other when Mrs. Di Maggio had seated them side by side on her first day. Neither one would talk during class, so they really didn't get to know each other until recess.

It was hard to start in a new school. The new term had already begun, and friendships were established. Many of the children had known one another from birth. Cliques were made, and Olivia was shy. She never knew how to start a conversation when she met people. She did much better playing with her toys—alone. Stella watched her, then walked over during recess in the school gym, easing into conversation as if they'd been friends for ages.

"Watch out for Jaden. He's very rough, and he'll try to take your schoolbag. My name's Stella. My dad calls me Stella Luna, but you can just call me Stella. Or you could call me Stella Luna. I know your name." Stella said all this in a rush as she pulled Olivia out of the way, before Jaden could mow them down. His manic chuckles echoed in the room.

"Why?" Olivia watched him move on, then turned her large amber eyes on the girl. Her hair felt too tight on her head. Her father's girlfriend braided the reddish-gold locks into braids that pulled at her tender scalp. She wanted to unplait them but didn't know how. Maybe Mommy would tell her not to do that again. Maybe she could write a note or something.

Stella had dark hair and chocolate-brown eyes to match her olive complexion. "Boys?" She shrugged. "Who knows what they're thinking."

Olivia agreed with a sage nod, thinking of her father. He was once a boy, so maybe he wasn't done being a boy yet. "How do you know that?"

"Oh, I've got plenty of them in m'house." She ticked them off with short, stubby fingers. "My father, my brother, a stepbrother, and now my new mother is having another baby. And guess what." She widened her eyes in astonishment. "It's another boy!"

"You're going to be outnumbered."

"No." Stella shook her head. "There are four of us girls and now four of them. I have a real sister and a step-sister. If they can stop having babies, I think we're safe. How many do you have?"

Olivia thought for a minute. Her father's new life was a raw wound to her. Instinctively, at home she didn't talk about it, wanting to make it easier for her mom. If she let herself think about it too much, she got a real deep feeling of hurt in the middle of her chest.

She opened her mouth, considering what to say. "Nope, no boys. Except if you consider my poppi. He just visits with my grandma."

"That doesn't count. Grandfathers are great. Where's your father? Is he dead? My real mommy died."

Olivia looked at Jaden, who was cartwheeling in a large circle in the gym, banging into children. She sighed heavily.

Stella touched her arm. "You don't have to tell me anything. In the end nothing matters."

Olivia wanted to tell Stella she was wrong. It did matter. It mattered a lot. She wisely kept her mouth shut, deciding a new friend was better than being right.

The next week, she went home with Stella. Her new mom was pregnant and had a baby girl named Christina. Olivia loved the baby's gummy smile. Mrs. Russo asked if they would watch her for an hour while she cooked dinner. Christina played on a crocheted blanket in the den. They made a game of throwing large rubber ducks, then acted like dogs retrieving them for the hysterical infant. They laughed just as much when she puffed out her chipmunk cheeks and waved her dimpled hands. She gurgled happily at their antics until two older boys brought in the smell of apples and wind when they entered the room. Olivia heard Mrs. Russo giving directions to Stella's teenaged sister about cooking in the kitchen.

A tug of war over a TV remote ruined the peaceful playroom, sending the baby into great gulping sobs. Stella gave a knowing look at the boys, who were fighting now over the PlayStation. She gestured to them with her firm little chin, as if to say, "See what I mean?"

Mrs. Russo snatched up the baby, grabbed the remote, and angrily shooed the boys from the room. The baby rested her head on her mother's strong shoulder, shuddering with relief.

"She's very intuitive," Stella assured Olivia, watching her mother place the baby in a walker.

"What, the baby?" Olivia said.

"Yeah, it means she can feel the change in the room when the *boys* come in. My father says I'm very intuitive."

"You are?" Olivia asked in wonder.

"Yep," Stella told her proudly, and then she lowered her voice. "I know when my mom is in the room."

Olivia looked through the entrance at Mrs. Russo, who was working at the stove in the kitchen.

"Not that one, my real mommy."

"The dead one?" Olivia whispered, her eyes wide.

"Yeah. Does your father come to visit you?" Stella was all business. Nothing rattled her.

Olivia thought for a minute, then answered, "Not enough."

"I can help you."

Olivia cast down her face sadly. "I don't know if I want to see him."

"Still mad?" Stella asked.

"Mad?"

"I was mad in the beginning." Stella guided her to her bedroom, where they sprawled on the shaggy rug. She picked up several Barbie dolls, their blond hair matted from years of greasy hands. They lined them up. "I was really mad, but then I had to help my dad."

"Why?"

"He was madder than me. We both couldn't be mad."

Olivia turned to look at her. "Why? Both my mommy and me are mad."

"Two mads are chaos."

"Kay-os. What's that?" Olivia lie on her back, holding Barbie and Ken above her, considering their frozen faces. She placed Ken facedown on the rug and played just with Barbie, whose blond hair swung in a tight ponytail.

"It's everything all messed up." Stella lie on her back, holding her hands in the air, making swirling motions. "Nothing gets done." Her voice was low. "Everybody fights; everybody's sad. I started wishing for my mommy to come and make it like it was."

"Did she?" Olivia stopped playing, turning on her side to face Stella. She rolled on top of Ken, fished him out, and tossed him into the toy box. She wasn't sure she wanted it back to the way it was.

"O'course. But she told me it can't go back to the old way. I had to learn to be happy with what I get."

"My daddy isn't dead."

"That's great!" Stella clapped her hands.

"He's just gone. He went with another lady and has a new baby."

"You'll get used to it," Stella told her grimly. "We all do."

"Do you like your new mommy?" Olivia asked. She wasn't crazy about her father's girlfriend, but the baby was fun.

"Uh-huh. She's great. I miss my mom, but now it's like I got two."

"I don't like Priscilla."

"That's a bad name."

"I know," Olivia agreed. "She's so mean."

Stella grew quiet, her eyes distant. She rose and walked over to an empty corner of the room. Weak light from the blinds striped her face in gold. She stared at the wall, as if listening intently. Olivia sat up, watchful, but could see nothing except the dust motes drifting on an invisible breeze. Nodding, she turned to Olivia.

"Don't worry about it. My mommy says the fun is just starting."

"Are you afraid?" Olivia asked, staring at the empty space.

"What? Of my mommy? Don't be silly."

"What if it's not your mommy?" Olivia whispered.

Stella considered her friend. She looked at the spot in the corner of the room. Turning to Olivia, she sighed. "Nope. Still not afraid."

Olivia stared at the wall, then back at Stella's face. Her friend looked fine. "Maybe everybody has one," she thought about the man she'd seen floating around her new house.

Olivia looked around the room again, searching for changing shadows. Then she shrugged and said, "Let's color."

* * *

Remy picked Olivia up before five thirty. She introduced herself to Ellie Russo. She liked her immediately. Ellie owned a small dance studio in town and warmly invited Remy to bring Olivia in for a class. Compact, with a nice-sized pregnancy going, she insisted Remy sit down for a cup of coffee. Ellie had short dark hair cut in a cap around her winsome face. Remy tried to guess her age but gave up. Her skin was rosy, her smile wide and inviting. It looked like she had a lot of kids running around the house.

"I didn't mind if she stayed for dinner," Ellie said as she set a huge table for seven people.

"How many kids do these people have?" Remy wondered, taking in the multiple places at the table and the scattered array of sneakers by the back door.

"We always have room for more. You could stay if you like." A teenaged girl was draining pasta. "Be careful, Veronica. Don't burn yourself." Remy looked at the girl, then at Ellie. Ellie smiled broadly, "Roni's my step daughter." She placed her arm around the younger girl's shoulders. "I adore her." She kissed the girl's blushing cheek. She gave her a squeeze and left her to finish the food.

Veronica smiled as she held the pot over a colander, expertly preparing the pasta for sauce.

"Thanks, but I have soup on the stove," Remy said. "It was so great meeting you. I'm planning a prenatal class, if you're interested."

"Count me in. My friend Molly just found out she's pregnant. She'll want to be included."

"Molly Valenti? The real estate broker? She's already enrolled."

"You know Molly? She's my husband's partner. Small world." They laughed. "I love your name: Remy. It's unusual."

"Not if your conception is due to a bottle of Remy Martin."

Ellie chuckled, looked at the teenager, and then said in a stage whisper. "I guess this baby ought to be called Dirty Martinis." She paused. "Drop off some flyers. I'll make sure my husband puts them in his office, and I'll leave them in the dance studio. You should pick up a lot of traffic there."

"I love this town. Everyone's been so nice."

She collected Olivia, promising they would return for a trip to the mall together the following week. She liked Ellie Russo. She loved the steamy kitchen and the sounds of children shrieking as they ran through the halls of the house. It was a mess of shoes, book bags, toys—a big, welcoming mess. It was a home.

She thought about the neat cottage and wondered what she could do to make it warmer for Olivia. She wanted her daughter to feel more comfortable in their home. Maybe they should start a collection, like perfume bottles. They could shop together. She brought it up to Olivia, who answered her absently.

"Did you have fun at your father's? She didn't braid your hair again, did she?"

Olivia shook her head. "Mom," Olivia said after a long moment. "How come you don't call him Daddy anymore?"

"What?" Remy glanced at her daughter in the back-seat. She lowered the news, which was droning on the radio. "What do you mean?"

"You used to call Daddy 'Daddy,' but now you just call him your father." Olivia paused. "And you say it mean."

"I'm sorry, honey. I guess I don't know. I think I'm still a little bit mad at your fa…at Daddy."

"Yeah. Two mads make kay-os, and then there's lots of fights. Can't have two mads," Olivia said in a rush.

"Well, you might be right, Olivia. Chaos would be a bad thing." She bit back a laugh. Remy thought for a minute. She didn't want Olivia caught in her battle. Olivia loved her father and had been dealt a low blow by the circumstances. Remy had no intention of dragging her into their fight. "So did you have fun at Daddy's?"

Olivia shrugged. "It was OK. I played with Evan."

Evan was her new baby brother.

Remy opened her eyes wide, hoping they wouldn't tear up. She didn't know if she'd ever be able to give her daughter another sibling. "What did you eat there?"

"Priscilla made meatballs." Olivia glanced up at her mother's face and spoke in earnest. "They weren't as good as yours."

Remy's eyes stung with those dreaded tears, but she smiled brightly at her daughter. Olivia turned her head to the window.

"Anything wrong?" Remy asked.

"No." Olivia stared outside at the scenery as they drove.

She was very quiet, too pensive.

"Did you have fun at Stella's?"

Olivia nodded.

"What did you do?" Remy thought that if her daughter gave her another one-word answer, she'd scream.

After a long sigh, Olivia said, "We talked."

"Talked," Remy repeated. "What did you talk about to Stella?"

"Nothing."

"Nothing? Did you play a game? What does she like? Did you have fun?"

"We talked about boys," Olivia said impatiently.

"Boys?" Remy echoed with shock as she looked intently at her daughter in the rearview mirror. "What could they have to say about boys," she wondered. She started to ask Olivia, but her daughter interrupted her.

"Mom, why do boys always want to ruin stuff?"

Remy opened her mouth but couldn't find words.

"You don't know either?" Olivia asked.

Remy giggled, then said, "I think they do things to get attention. Boys do things to girls because they like them, and that's the way they get the girls to notice them. Did a boy do something to you?"

"No. Does that mean that Daddy wants you to notice him?"

Remy's tongue froze in her mouth. "I just don't know what your father wanted, Livie." She needed to change the subject. "I made pudding. You want pudding after dinner?"

The rest of the ride was in thoughtful silence. Remy worried her bottom lip.

Remy parked the car behind the house in its spot. They made a mad dash for the door, the freezing snow crunching under their feet. Olivia looked up, awed by the black-velvet night sky dotted with sparkling pinpoints of light.

"Mom, look!"

They watched a shooting star arcing across the darkness, leaving a cosmic trail of silver.

"Make a wish," Remy urged. She watched her daughter's pale face look up, wondering what her heart was hoping for. "What was your wish?"

They held hands as they trudged through the snow toward the kitchen door. "Can't tell. If I do, it won't come true." Olivia wanted this wish to come true. She didn't know how it could, but she just wanted her mommy to smile more. Clouds of frost appeared before her tiny mouth. Remy helped her up the three icy stone steps to the back door. She reminded herself she'd have to pick up salt in the hardware store, as she climbed carefully.

Remy slid off her glove to unlock the door. The house was completely dark. She touched the switch at the entrance, but the lights didn't work. It was as cold as it was dark. Their breaths froze in the night air before them. Remy bent down, holding Olivia by the shoulders and peering directly into her eyes to make sure she understood.

"Wait here. Don't move until I come back for you."

She entered the room, her hands freezing. The heat was off. This was crazy. The floor was littered with broken shards of glass that glistened in the light of the full moon that glowed through the window. Remy used her cell phone to light the way to the breaker board in the hallway.

"Sing to me, Olivia," she called out to her daughter.

She smiled when the faint sound of "You Are My Sunshine" echoed back from the kitchen. Holding one hand against the smooth wall, she felt her way into the parlor. Blinking hard into the darkness, Remy paused, the hair on the back of her neck rising. A small orb floated over the fireplace. Her heart beat wildly in her chest. She closed her eyes fiercely, then reopened them, expecting to see nothing there. But it was still there, floating along the mantle, coming toward her.

"Olivia!" Remy shouted, her back pressed against the wall, her knees locked.

"Do you want me to sing louder, Mommy?" Her daughter's reassuring voice made her feel silly and relieved at the same time.

The light dissolved, leaving Remy to laugh shakily. "Yes, please," she called out, her voice high. "Livie, sing it again." It had to be a reflection, she reasoned.

Remy's hand found the switch, and she flipped the breakers. She was pleased when the light flooded the room. Her sigh of pleasure turned to dismay when she noticed the wreck in her living room. Her eyes circled the area, catching the great orb of light again. Remy gasped and squinted. She turned her flashlight on it, and it faded into the brightness.

"Can I stop singing now, Mommy?" Olivia called.

Remy's mouth hung open as she searched the room, wondering if she really saw anything at all. Olivia's impatient voice called, "Mommy! Can I stop singing?"

"Yes," she answered in a shocked voice, and then she repeated it louder with more confidence. She didn't want to worry Olivia. The chairs in the parlor had been overturned. Books were strewn across the floor. Feathers from her pillows wafted down the staircase to land on the wooden floors. She backed out of the door, grabbing Olivia's hand as she made a beeline for her car, slipping just a bit on those blasted steps. Regaining her balance, she raced across the cobbles, throwing Olivia into the front seat.

"Wait, Mommy! I don't have my seatbelt on!" Olivia wailed.

Remy heard herself huffing, her breath coming in quick gasps. "Hurry, baby, just do it quickly."

She pulled sharply out of her driveway, raced to the center of town, a mere block away, and called the police.

They arrived eight minutes later and followed her back home to search the house.

The officer scratched his head with puzzlement. "Are you sure you left the door locked?"

"Absolutely, Officer Finley." She looked around the carnage in her kitchen. Bending down, she picked up the needlepoint her mother had made for her daughter. "I don't understand this. They didn't take anything."

"Does your ex-husband have a key?"

"No…no, of course not."

"Well, keep the doors locked," he said as he finished his report. He handed her a yellow slip of paper. "Call if you see anything suspicious."

"Like floating orbs," Remy thought, but she chose not to mention them. It had to be a trick of light.

Remy and her daughter stared at the messy floor. Flour was spilled on the counter. A planter had been overturned, the dirt sprayed across the floor.

"Boys." Olivia's mouth pursed into a disapproving line.

"What?" Remy turned to her.

"The only one who could have done this is a boy. The question is, Mommy, which boy wants us to notice him?"

Remy locked the door, then swept up the kitchen first so she could feed her daughter. She walked from room to room, turning on every lamp in the small house.

"Why are you putting on all the lights?" Olivia stayed close to her.

"It's much nicer when it's bright, right, Livie?"

They ate soup and tuna sandwiches in silence. Olivia propped her head on her hand, looking irate. Her rosebud mouth was pursed, her brows wrinkled over her serious eyes.

"It's nothing, honey. Just a prankster or something."

"What's a prankster?"

"Someone who likes to joke," Remy said.

Olivia's little face was glum. "Well, I don't think this is very funny." She pushed away her plate. "I'm done."

"No, you're not. Livie, finish your food."

Her daughter showed her a decidedly mutinous pout. Remy could see an epic meltdown heading their way. She had seen it coming for a few days now, with the move, the new school, going to her father's. Olivia kept things to herself and had a mostly amiable demeanor, but she had a formidable temper that lurked below the surface. "It must have come from Scott's side of the family," Remy thought with chagrin.

Remy looked directly at her and told her sternly, "You're asking for a time-out, Olivia."

Olivia shook her head. Her lips thinned. Tears brimmed in her eyes. Her bottom lip quivered ominously.

Remy sighed loudly, her chest tight with anxiety. It was all going to fall on her own shoulders now. She was a single mom. Would Olivia stumble into the cracks with other kids who were trouble? Not enough parental guidance. No more good cop, bad cop. Her tag team of discipline was gone—not that it functioned really well in the past year. That's when the whole thing fell apart.

She watched her daughter war with her feelings and consider the half-eaten sandwich. Finally she pulled her plate back to give her mother the victory.

"Good choices. I love it when you make good choices, Olivia. I'm very proud of you."

Remy changed the subject to the upcoming winter concert in school. She took down the extra bedding she kept for guests, and redressed the mussed beds. She tucked Olivia in after her two stories and a bedtime song.

With a broom and a mop, she spent the next forty minutes cleaning the mess in her parlor. When she entered her study, she found her new television hanging from its arm, the glass shattered.

"Why, Scott?" she asked the empty room, knowing he was the only one who could possibly do such a thing. But why would he want her to notice him?

Eli watched the woman clean the mess, feeling his face tighten with shame. He hadn't meant to be so destructive. He didn't know what had come over him. He wanted to scare them a bit, just enough to make them leave. Having them here made him uncomfortable, brought back strange feelings. The child stared at the spot where he levitated as she climbed the steps to her room. Her eyes narrowed with anger, filling him with dread. She unnerved him, she did.

CHAPTER SIX

O livia didn't know what woke her, but her eyes opened to scan the darkness of the room. Protectively, she tucked the great blue whale she slept with under her arm. She petted his furry head attentively. Olivia sat up, then slid out of the pink confection of a bed. Her toes sank into the raspberry shag carpet as she approached the wall.

Eli sat on the top of her dresser, watching the girl's movements as she walked around the room. His eyes glittered in the dark.

"Wait for it. Wait for it," he told himself. He planned on putting her in her place. It was time to take back his territory. He opened his mouth to roar.

Olivia's little fingers grazed the walls as she circled slowly in his direction. He had filled himself up with air, ready to unleash a blast of icy wind, when her chubby but determined fingers settled on his calf, squeezing his skin until he howled like a little girl.

"Ow…ow…ow…"

Olivia twisted again, causing Eli to rear up in pain, wondering how in the world she was able not only to find him but to touch him. Making a fist, she punched hard, this time slamming him in his groin, reminding him of a long-forgotten part of his body. He curled into a ball and rolled onto the floor.

"Olivia, you OK?" Her mom's muffled call floated up the staircase.

"I'm fine, Mom," she shouted, taking her petite foot and kicking him in the bread basket. "That's for making a mess," she hissed.

Eli groaned, holding himself, then croaked, "Who told you to hit a person there?"

"My poppi. Who are you?" Her amber eyes peered down at him intently, her little brow furrowed with anger. Eli might have laughed if it didn't hurt so much. She was a miniature of the woman downstairs, but a termagant if he'd ever seen one.

"You're going to make some guy's life a living hell one day, princess." He crawled to be nose to nose with her. "Aren't you afraid of me?"

Olivia mutely shook her head. "Are you the captain? Do you know Stella's mom?" Olivia peered closely at his face.

"Who's Stella?" he asked, watching her just as closely. Maybe the couple in the shiny clothes could scare her, but he sure as hell wasn't doing much. "How did you know I was a captain?"

"The painting in the living room. Do you live here too?" She kept up her rapid-fire questions. "Are you doing this because you like my mother?"

"Like your mother?" Eli asked incredulously.

"Are you trying to get her attention?" Olivia thought for a minute. "You know, you are not making good choices."

"Good choices?"

"You're asking for a time-out," Olivia said as she climbed back into her frilly bed.

"Time-out?" Eli wondered what she was talking about but found himself following her.

"I'm tired. You have to do something else, because she was really mad about the mess."

"Mess?" Eli asked, bending over the bed.

"Yes, the mess. As if you didn't know," she muttered. Olivia reached for the covers. "I can't get them. Can you hand them to me?"

Eli stood open mouthed, his hands slack at his sides.

"The covers, please?" Olivia said.

Without knowing why, Eli found himself tucking her in, a memory tickling at the back recesses of his mind. He watched her eyes drift shut. They widened as the little girl fought sleep. "I forgot to ask, what's your name?"

He thought for a minute, reaching for the information. It had been so long, he wasn't quite sure he could even say it. But he did. "Eli, Captain Eli Gaspar." He bent low, close to her face.

"Captain Eli. That's a funny name." Olivia patted his cheek. "Did you catch the whale?"

This was crazy, the world was upside down. He had to think of something to get the upper hand. After all, who was in command of this ship? He was going to have to pull out all the stops and show this halfling who was in charge. Using all his energy, he turned transparent, his skin sliding off, leaving him a skeleton, his eye sockets empty but for worms. It was no use. The imp of Satan was snoring softly.

Eli sat down on the carpet, humiliated. He had lost his touch. Too many years of comfortable existence with Pat. He was rusty, couldn't scare a six-year-old. What was happening to him? He stared at her red-gold hair fanned out across the pillow. Taking a curl between his fingers, he caressed it. It was baby soft, like down.

The room clouded, and distant cries of seagulls filled the air. The ocean pounded against the shore, and the room faded into sepia-toned hues spangled with gold.

CHAPTER SEVEN

1838

"**W**ake up, Princess Charlotte." Eli Gaspar nuzzled the petal softness of his daughter's cheek. "Wake up, my sweet girl."

"Eli. Eli, is she up?" a musical voice called from downstairs. "Really, Eli, we'll be late for church."

They could hear the bells of Saint John's in the distance, calling parishioners to the Sunday services.

Charlotte stretched widely and opened sleepy blue eyes.

"Papa!" She jumped up and threw herself at Eli, who caught her deftly.

He stood to his full height, his dark head grazing the low beams of the whitewashed ceiling. "Wisht, you little powder monkey." He pulled off the sleeping cap that covered her bouncing curls. "You must have grown a foot," he groaned, swaying as if she were too heavy to carry.

"I mithed you!" Charlotte revealed a gap-toothed smile that sent Eli into whoops of laughter.

"What happened to your teeth, kitten?"

"Marcus hit me in the fath and knocked out my tooth."

"I'll keelhaul the little bastard." His face darkened.

"No, no, Papa. He didn't do it on purposth. He did it 'cause he likth me," she explained, as if he were an idiot.

"What do you mean?"

"Eli!" Sarah called from the bottom step. "Eli, I can't make the steps today. Please don't make me climb the steps."

Eli and Charlotte exchanged guilty glances. He dropped her on the feather bed. "Come on, shark bait. We better get moving before your mother gets upset and has the baby early."

Charlotte threw on her dress, and Eli deftly buttoned up the back. They clamored down the steps, Charlotte on his back, Eli leaping off the last step to his daughter's delight.

"Eli, the noise, please," Sarah implored, her hand at her temple.

He had just gotten home from a six-week trip. Both he and his father-in-law had met their investors in Connecticut. He had struggled so to get here, his first command. He had served as second mate for the past seven years. Because he was working hard, he had missed every milestone from his honeymoon to the birth of his daughter, Charlotte, over the past half-dozen years or so. It was a hard life, but he loved it and saw great potential in it.

They had scrimped and saved, and with his father-in-law's help, his dream had just become a reality. His profit, along with the money Sarah's father invested, made up for half of the cost of the twenty-thousand-dollar *Mattie*

McGee, a neat little hundred-foot bark. Eli was excited—his first command. He swung his daughter around to land in a ruffled mess on the floor.

"Gertie, get Charlotte's spencer ready. Go on," said Sarah. "Get in the trap with Gertie, and I'll meet you there."

Charlotte ran after their cook to get her outer clothing and leave. Sarah turned to place her small hand on Eli's chest. She pressed her big belly against his side. Eli wrapped his arms around his wife. The amber earbobs he'd purchased on his last trip winked in the sunlight pouring in through the spotless windows.

"Do you have to leave so soon?" she pleaded. "The baby is due in just a few weeks."

He kissed her gently on her soft mouth. "This won't be a long trip."

She eyed him distrustfully. "You said that the last time, and it was four years."

"Come on, Sarah. I've been hugging the coast for the last few years, taking in small loads. That trip was years ago."

It was still a bone of contention between them, sorely testing their relationship. He had left soon after they married for a four-year trip, making them enough to start their life together and purchase this little cottage. In her defense, he shipped out not knowing she was pregnant. If not for her parents, who lived up the hill, she would have lost her mind.

After he returned and saw how she had suffered in his absence, he selected local jobs that took him away for shorter periods, but he didn't make as much. He missed the open sea and the opportunities of better fishing. Sarah hated the whaling. She despised the odor that clung to him, the danger he put himself into. With her mother dying earlier this year, Sarah became more unreasonable. She was weepy, difficult, but a man had to support his family.

"We need the money. I have to do this for your father, Sarah. He's put up eight thousand dollars. I owe it to him."

"What about me?" she demanded. "You just got back." Sarah rested her head against his chest, and a tear slid down her face. Eli hated when she cried. It always started with delicate sniffles and grew into dramatic sobs. She was a wee bit spoiled. Her father spoiled her, Eli spoiled her. He couldn't help it. Sarah was special. She wasn't cut out to be a whaler's wife. She had grown up with finer things. As the daughter of a prominent attorney, she was used to her comfort. She never missed a chance to let him know what she thought of his career choice. She wanted him to open a shop or work in one of the many mills.

Eli loved the sea and all that went with it. There was nothing more exciting than chasing whales all over the world. He had a chance here to change their lives. He made it up to his wife by stretching his budget and hiring both a cook and a tweeny—a little servant girl to clean the fireplaces, do the slops. It reduced the portion for his own needs. He wore old boots and a secondhand coat, but Sarah had what she needed. He looked down at her rosy complexion, framed by golden curls. She had dark blue eyes, rimmed with black lashes that could capture his attention without a word being said. He kissed her upturned nose, the dewy skin making him wish his daughter would go to church with Gertie and give him a few precious hours with the love of his life. He knew she loved him just as fiercely, and she had thought she understood his life when they wed.

That was the lot of a whaler's wife. It wasn't easy, but it was the best opportunity for a poor boy from Long Island. His parents owned only enough land to help their older son, his brother Jacob. There was nothing left for Eli, not that it mattered. He had no head for farming, never had. He fished the harbor for years, selling oysters and clams to the Milleridge Inn. He got his first job at sixteen on a fishing boat. He made it to first mate by the time he married Sarah, shipping out on that long trip weeks after they married. It was one of the first to depart out of Cold Spring, but he made good money and was able to buy the small house for his little family without the help of her father.

When Charlotte was born while he was at sea, he decided to change ships, taking quick runs instead, learning the waters of the North Atlantic, where they picked up blackfish and small pilot whales. They were easy to catch, yielding profitable quantities of oil, and hunting them trained him for the bigger prey in deeper waters. He flexed the muscles of his forearm. It was hard work, filthy, but it had the potential to make him a good life. They saved and saved, enabling him to buy in as a partner on the bark with his father-in-law and a couple of big shots from Connecticut.

He was a merchant now and didn't have to rely on his brawn. Soon he'd have a fleet of ships, he assured his wife. They would move to one of the bigger houses on the hill and have lots of servants. Couldn't she see this time as an investment in their future? He and Sarah had both grown up in the town. She was educated at home, and he had attended West Side School, established in 1790. George Washington himself had set the rafters in that school. While he had gotten a fair education, a clerk job was not for him. His son would go to that school and maybe become a lawyer like his grandfather.

Eli was an important part of the community now, not just another tar on a whaleboat. He was a captain, a businessman like Fred Allen, who ran the paper mill, or Josiah Banks, who owned the flour mill. He lived in a town that was being noticed because of whaling. The natural harbor made it important. He loved the little village, now bustling with excitement caused by the Jones brothers. They had invested in a whole fleet and were on their way to putting Cold Spring on the map. There was a need for whale products, and they lived in the center of the world right now. They had to take a chance.

"Don't you see, Sarah?" He held her away at arm's length, looking at her piquant, heart-shaped face. "We finally caught the great wave. The Joneses understand what a perfect gift our little harbor is. They are buying a fleet, Sarah! A fleet of whaling ships all leaving from here. Already people are moving in—barrel makers, sailors, merchants, chandlers—all to feed this new industry."

"We don't need it," Sarah replied petulantly. "The Hewlett-Jones grist mill provides plenty of work. What do you need to kill all those poor whales for?" She stuck out her lower lip. "I don't care if I live in a root cellar if it means you'll stay home. Eli, I miss you dreadfully." Her face turned blotchy, and he knew tears simmered beneath the surface of her smoldering blue eyes. He hated when she cried. It twisted him all up, staying with him long after he went to sea.

Trying to distract her, Eli spun her around to a lamp hanging in the corner of the parlor. "Poor whales? Like reading late into the evening? Whale oil is progress, Sarah mine. Whale oil lets us work into the evenings, get more things done. It helps us grow." Eli's dark eyes gleamed with excitement. "The oil lubricates the machines that made the cotton for your dress." He picked up a dainty parasol resting on the table, opening it with a snap. "Why, the spokes for your little umbrella are made from whalebone. The city of New Bedford is already being called the 'City That Lights the World.' No part of the beast is wasted. The spermaceti from the whale's head is used to make smokeless candles. Don't you want to be part of this new age, Sarah? I don't want to haul sacks of flour until my back breaks." His dark eyes implored her. "Sarah, if I don't do it, someone else will. Sweeting, I want you to live in luxury."

"No, you want to go chasing after your adventures whilst I stay here and give birth to your son!" She rested her hand on her bulging belly. "Charlotte hardly knows you." The threatened tears spilled. She was not a pretty crier. The color traveled down to her neck until everything from hairline to bodice was beet red.

Eli pulled her close. "Charlotte knows her papa very well." He kissed her nose gently. "I didn't want to leave you pregnant, Sarah. I didn't want to the last time, and I don't now. I have little choice in the matter."

Sarah sniffed resentfully, her eyes downcast.

Guilt assailed him. She was in a delicate condition. He had no right to make these demands on her, yet so many women did it without complaint. Why couldn't she make it easier? His heart was breaking too. He tipped up her chin, whispering against her lips.

"I mean to make you a wealthy woman. I owe a responsibility to your father. I have a job to do, Sarah." He grazed the tops of her ample breast with the pads of his fingers. Lowering his fingers into her bodice, he caressed the whalebone busk sewn into her garment, close to her heart.

"I love you, Sarah. You are my life." He touched the busk, his eyes gazing into hers. "Haven't I carved those words to lay next to your heart?"

"And the two shall become one flesh." Sarah whispered the private words Eli had carved onto her busk during his last voyage, for her eyes only. All the sailors did it for their sweethearts. The women sewed the whalebone busks into their chemise to wear close to their hearts. Their hands entwined over the busk.

"One flesh, Sarah mine." He bent down to kiss her, their tongues dancing in the age-old movement of passion. "I will not be gone four years this time. I will be back within eighteen months. It'll go fast, I promise."

"Mama!" Charlotte called from outside. "Thaint Johnth ith ringing the bellth again. We will be late."

Eli laughed at his daughter's lisp. "It's bad. I hardly understand her."

"By the time you come back, she'll have all her adult teeth," Sarah said pertly, her eyes sparking.

Eli wrapped his wife's cape around her shoulders. "I love you, Sarah. I love our family. I wouldn't do this if I had a choice."

Sarah grabbed her reticule with resignation. She wanted to tell him everyone had choices. They just made different ones.

CHAPTER EIGHT

Cold Spring Harbor, 2014

"Heard you had a break-in last week." A man stood in the entry of her studio, shaking the dusting of snow from the slouchy hat he wore. He tugged off his glove with very straight, white teeth while he stamped the powdery snow from his feet on the mat outside the door.

"Excuse me?" Remy walked over gracefully, holding her broom so tightly her knuckles turned white. She was barefoot and the cold air made her toes go numb. She curled them up. "Do I know you?"

She tilted her head, looking at him hard. The air seemed to thin, and her breath hitched. Once, when she was about Olivia's age, she had fallen from a treehouse. The ground had rushed up to knock the air from her body. She had the same breathless feeling now. The world tilted, just a bit, and she lost her center.

Pausing, she inhaled deeply, counting in her head, restoring her equilibrium. She stared at his face, feeling something, as if the atmosphere had gelled around them.

"Well, no, no, really, and…" He backed away at her aggressive stance. "Are you quite all right? I'm not going to hurt you." He held up his hands defensively. "Your mother suggested I stop by."

"My mother?"

He extended a long, tanned hand. "Hugh Matthews. How do you do?" He had a slight British accent, just enough to let you know he'd spent some time there. He filled the small studio with his height. He wasn't big like Scott, but more lanky, with an endearing awkwardness, as though he hadn't grown into his body yet. His brown hair was long, bordering on shaggy, and he flipped it back with a wave of his head. Penetrating slate eyes watched her intently, but it was his well-shaped lips that drew her gaze. He had the sexiest lips she had ever seen on a man.

Remy caught herself staring as he spoke, realizing she was gawking like a horny teenager.

"You're from England?"

"No, no, my mother was born there. They sent me to my grandparents for the summers growing up. I'm afraid it's all her fault. Does the accent bother you?" He looked down at her, his gaze intent. "Can I come in?"

"No," Remy blushed, then laughed. "I mean, yes, you can come in, and no, your accent doesn't bother me. I didn't mean to be rude." The air crystallized in frosty clouds when she spoke.

Hugh shifted from one foot to the other, his clear gray eyes assessing her. Remy smoothed the wild curls, wishing she had blown them out this morning rather than let them air dry into a tumbleweed mass. Absently, she brushed at a spec on her cheek, smearing the smudge to cover her cinnamon colored freckles.

"Charming, not rude." Hugh smiled, causing a sea of butterflies to erupt in Remy's midsection. Remy got flustered, dropping the broom. They both reached for it, and their heads collided with a loud whack.

"Oops," said Remy.

"So sorry. I'm clumsy."

"No, it's my fault," Remy said as they wrestled with the broomstick, then looked at each other, smiling shyly.

Hugh held his hands up in the air. "I give up. You win." He cocked his head. "I meant to come by sooner, but I've been busy with some antiques that have been donated." It sounded like a lame excuse, and they both knew it. He was here because her mother had bugged him to come. Remy rubbed the sore spot on her forehead where they'd collided, her face red with embarrassment. She pressed down so hard on the broom that the bristles bent.

Hugh cleared his throat in the uncomfortable silence. "Looks like you're between classes. Would you like to get a drink?"

Remy looked at the clock. "It's eleven o'clock in the morning."

"It doesn't have to be alcohol." Hugh grinned, looking like a boy. Remy's breath stilled in her chest. "Tea shop's right down the street. Starbucks is around the corner, if you prefer."

"Did my mother put you up to this?" Remy asked baldly, then gasped at her boldness.

Hugh smiled a lazy grin, then laughed. "Well…yes. Not very polite of me to admit, but I believe honesty is the best policy." He paused, his eyes dancing with mirth. "I have to say that I'm glad I finally took the time to meet you. What about that drink?"

"I…" Remy reached in her mind for an excuse. Any number of things popped into her head, but the appealing gray eyes made her reconsider for a minute. Hugh waited expectantly. Remy reconsidered her first response. There was no reason she shouldn't go. "I'll get my coat."

They walked down Main Street, making sure there was a polite distance between them. Every so often, Hugh reached over to take her elbow, helping her over the ice remaining on the frozen sidewalk.

"They're supposed to put salt out," he said.

Remy smiled, wondering why he acted as though it was his responsibility. She nodded at his small talk, moving a shade closer to hear his smooth voice. He gave her a commentary about the tidy shops they passed, pausing here and there to point out something of interest. It was clear he loved the town and all its inhabitants. Remy found it sweet, and interrupted occasionally to ask a pertinent question. Several times she noticed the various shopkeepers wave to him in a friendly matter.

He stopped a time or two, shaking hands, asking a question, but overall it appeared the man was simply adored by everybody. She expected bluebirds and butterflies to hover over his head while angels sang. It was really too much. She wished she had worn her new yoga pants, the ones that hugged her body, rather than the tired ones she had on. Hunching her shoulders, she made herself small, feeling unlovely next to this lovely man.

Hugh held the door open. He ducked ever so slightly when they entered the cozy tea shop. The bell announced their arrival. Hugh placed his hand on her back and led her to a small table. Remy's skin sizzled when he touched her, and her face reddened. He was greeted warmly by the proprietor, a heavyset woman with a belly as large as her chest. The woman insisted they move to a bigger table, covered with flowered chintz, near the counter.

Remy sat quietly listening as Hugh chattered away with Mrs. Travis, discussing the drainage problem troubling Main Street. It was the same place she had met her parents a few weeks ago. Every so often, Mrs. Travis would narrow her beady eyes, as if she were measuring Remy, only to find her a poor specimen. She wished she could disappear into the cabbage rose wallpaper.

Hugh informed her the shop had been in operation for almost a hundred years. They made all their own treats and served a traditional British tea. Finally, Mrs. Travis excused herself to natter with another regular about her grandchildren.

They sat opposite each other, and Remy took off her coat. She turned to face him and noticed a perfect bruise forming on his forehead. Her brow furrowed with dismay. "Did I do that?" She laughed, reaching out to caress the mark.

"You have a matching one." His fingers grazed her forehead. Embarrassed, she evaded his hand. Tea arrived, this time from a sullen-faced blonde of about twenty-three. She placed the three-tiered plate of tiny sandwiches with a thud, glared at Remy, then sashayed back to the counter.

"Mrs. Travis's niece. I'm afraid she's nursing a rather horrible crush. I'm hungry," Hugh said, piling half the sandwiches on his plate.

Remy looked after the girl, who now stared daggers in her back.

"Should I be afraid to eat?" she asked Hugh.

"What? Oh, Cynthia. No, don't worry. She knows I'm too old for her. She's fourteen."

"Fourteen? She looks older."

Hugh shrugged. "Not wiser. She quit school. I got her into a work program at the library in Huntington. She'll be fine."

Hugh explained he worked at the museum on a grant, which was funded by a big corporation. He had a history degree, which he admitted was pretty much useless. She listened intently, staring at his mouth shaping each word. A thick silence made her realize the lips had asked a question. Remy squirmed, backtracking the conversation, wondering what in the hell he asked her.

Taking a shot in the dark, she cleared her throat, muttering that there wasn't much for a degree in communications either. She looked up to find his gray eyes dancing with amusement, and she wondered if he knew what distracted her. She realized he was talking about dinner.

"Dinner. I asked if you would like to go for dinner Friday."

"Um…"

"It's not a trick question. We'll eat, and then talk some more. I promise you're going to like it," he said.

Remy placed her used napkin on the plate and rose to her feet. "Thanks." She held out her hand. "It was nice meeting you. I, um…I'm newly single, you see. It's been a long time, and…I don't think I'm ready."

"How long?" Hugh asked gently.

"What?" she asked, her voice slightly raised. All talking had stopped. Remy looked around apologetically, repeating, "What?" in a lower voice.

"When did you divorce? How long have you been single? I make it a habit not to be the rebound guy."

Remy stiffened. "How often have you been the rebound guy?"

"Often enough to know it's not pleasant."

"Well, I guess that's that." She shoved the chair under the table and turned to leave.

"What do you mean? I got the feeling from your mother that it's been a while," Hugh said as he stood. "I don't know why I didn't run when we banged heads in your studio. Not an auspicious start to our relationship, head butting." He laughed.

"Who said anything about a relationship?" she demanded hotly.

"Oh no, our first fight," he said with a smile. "Come on. That was funny."

An unexpected chuckle bubbled up from her throat. He was absurd, but in a good way.

Remy opened her mouth to say good-bye but found the words wouldn't come. It was funny. He was funny, made her laugh. It was as though her mouth and head lost connection. Remy sighed in resignation and told him, "It's been close to a year." She didn't like to talk about it but found herself slipping into a comfortable feeling with him. She struggled with her coat. It was hooked on the arm of her chair and she couldn't get it off. "I am such a nerd," she said with exasperation.

"How close?" Hugh easily lifted her coat off the back of her chair, then helped her into it. He squeezed her shoulders reassuringly.

"Eleven months, three weeks," she said. She almost added five days, but her tongue instinctively stopped before she could utter it. She pressed her fingers to her temple. This was hard, meeting someone new. She wasn't good at it when she was younger. She might as well hang a sign around her neck that said something like "loony tune ex-wife who can't let go." Or, "the rejected one."

Next he was going to ask why. She knew it. What could she say? That she wasn't enough for Scott, so he had to look elsewhere? She enraged her husband enough to strike her. He preferred another woman's bed. He was in his new relationship for almost two and a half years with a Hooters waitress who looked happy enough. Why was it working for them and not for her? She had been so sure of Scott. Could she ever trust herself again? Maybe they should put a sticker on her bumper asking people to call to report bad wifing. She frowned, her face lost thought. She wanted to scream at him, "Run, I'm not normal yet," but the words died on her lips. She paused, looking up at his concerned face. He stood quietly, considering her, respecting the silence between them. There was no pity in his face, and he didn't ask why Scott left. He patiently watched her struggle, then smiled encouragingly. Ice melted in Remy's heart. They stared at each other, sounds around them muted, as though they were alone. Remy took a deep breath, allowing it to cleanse her soul. The serenity felt good—for both of them.

"I think it's long enough," Hugh said softly. "Maybe it's time to join the living."

"I thought you didn't want to be the rebound guy," Remy said, turning to look up at him. He had his hands in his pockets. Remy suddenly had the insight that he wasn't all that comfortable either. It was liberating.

"I don't plan to be. Just a dinner," he said simply.

Remy looked at his lips, wondering why she couldn't agree. She crushed the growing attraction into a hard little ball, tucking it away to dissect later. Even though it was for Friday, and she knew she would be free, she told him no. Olivia was spending the weekend with Scott and Prunella. She couldn't do it. Shaking her head, her eyes downcast, she bade him good-bye. She was not ready to go out on a date yet.

CHAPTER NINE

Remy started for the door to head back to work, annoyed with herself. She felt seventeen again, gawky, an uncoordinated mess. She wondered if Hugh had noticed it. He insisted on escorting her back to the studio. They strolled in silence. Every so often, their arms brushed each other. Once again, Hugh reached out to help her navigate the icy patches.

At first she edged away, but he moved closer, making her feel protected. "Give in to it. Don't be afraid," she thought, making a mantra in her head. They barely spoke, but the lack of conversation didn't feel awkward. If anything, it felt comfortable.

"Didn't I lock the door when I left?" she asked, picking up her pace on the sidewalk.

"I'm not sure," Hugh said increasing his stride to keep up with her. A group of people were milling around the sidewalk leading to her studio.

Remy started to trot, taking in the crowd in front of the walkway of her studio. They had to go down a narrow path, since the door was in the alley between two buildings.

"What happened?" Remy called out.

"Someone broke the windows. There's smoke coming out of the storefront." A man pointed to her entrance.

Remy started to run, but Hugh's large hand pulled her back.

"Slow down. Did anyone call the police?" he asked the crowd with authority.

"Police and fire departments," said someone in the crowd.

"Ah, here they come," Hugh said. Sirens filled the air, which had turned bitter cold. Hugh touched her elbow. "Come into the church."

"I don't want to go to church." Remy was annoyed. "I have to see what's going on." She was concerned, her attraction to Hugh moved to the nether spaces of her brain.

"Sam." Hugh nodded to an officer walking briskly toward them. "Any idea what happened?"

The cop nodded, and his partner dispersed the crowd as a spanking new fire truck pulled up, with eager firemen pulling out a hose to clamp onto the hydrant.

"What are you, the mayor or something?" Remy demanded testily. She was worried about her studio.

Hugh's face turned crimson, and his feet shuffled. "As a matter of fact, um…yes. Come on. It's cold. We'll wait inside."

"I can't." She craned her neck around him to see her studio. "It's all I have. I have to see if the studio is all right."

Hugh rested his warm hands over hers. "Sam, can we get closer?"

The officer bade them to wait until he had checked it out, and then he motioned for them to move through the crowd to the entrance. Broken glass littered the sidewalk. Hugh took Remy's hand and led her to her studio. Firemen milled around the small space.

"It didn't catch," the fire chief stated, pointing to a small charred cloth that smoked on the floor. They gathered around it. Hugh crouched next to a policeman, who poked it with his club.

"Looks like something a kid would do." They all looked up at Remy

She shrugged. "What do you mean?"

"It's a rock soaked in turpentine. Some kid lit it and threw it at the window." The officer considered Remy. "Is there anyone who has a gripe with you? A landscaper? Boyfriend?"

Remy shook her head mutely. "When can I clean it up? I have clients coming at four."

"It seems you've doubled the crime in Cold Spring Harbor," Hugh told her with mock seriousness. He turned to the policeman. "You are calling in detectives?"

"Yeah. They plan on joining us after they finish chasing the Canadian Geese off the library roof," the officer said snidely. "It shouldn't be longer than an hour." The policeman looked at Hugh. "They may have a few questions."

"All right, then." He stood and straightened his long legs. "You'll find us at my office."

The cold was seeping through the thin soles of Remy's shoes, making her toes numb. She let Hugh take her hand again. Instantly she snatched her fingers from his grasp.

"I'm not easy," she said. Then she covered her mouth. "Oh, my God. I don't know what—"

"It's OK." Hugh smiled. "I am."

CHAPTER TEN

The small church was just a little larger than her own studio. The ceiling arched upward toward a vaulted roof. Hugh explained that it was built in the Greek Revival style, which meant nothing to Remy. All she noticed was that the walls were whitewashed a shabby chic, and the interior was rather plain. Each wall was taken up with rows of locally made furniture.

Six or eight display cases took the place of the pews. They were staggered, placed in a chevron style, so that you saw a little bit of each artifact across the room. Folk art pictures of locals, their faces frozen in time, stared back from the top portion of the tall walls. Remy blew on her hands while Hugh checked his thermostat.

"It's an old building, but I promise you'll be warm in a minute," he said. "I don't know why it's so cold."

"Why?" Remy looked up at him.

"Why is it so cold, or why am I mayor?" Hugh shrugged. "I'm a trust fund baby. Do you know what that means? Ah, I see that you don't. There are generations of money, seven in fact, put away for my use. I refused to go into banking like my father and his father before that."

He pulled out a folding chair for her. "I love history. Any history. So I bought this church. They were going to turn it into a clothing store, so I purchased all these artifacts, and voila." He snapped his long fingers. "I turned it into a museum. I'm a major contributor. The town was having an election and asked me to run." Hugh had the grace to blush. "I never expected to win," he said, sounding faintly embarrassed.

"Mayor Matthews." Remy curtsied.

"Just Hugh, ma'am." He leaned against a display case. "Can't I get you something to drink?"

"Please." Remy placed her palms on her flat stomach. "Any more, and I'll float away." She turned to the door as if to leave. "What's taking them so long?" She bit her lower lip. She walked down the aisle, rubbing her hands against her arms. "Is this where the pulpit was?" she called back to him.

Hugh nodded with a smile. "The left side."

Remy strolled closer, and a chill danced up her spine. Cool air eddied in a tiny whirlpool, making her shiver. She looked back at Hugh. "You have a draft here."

He strolled toward her, feeling the temperature drop significantly. "That's strange. I never noticed it before." He looked up for a hole in the vaulted roof, then walked over to the radiator, placing his hand on the return. "Come closer to the heat."

"Said the spider to the fly," she thought. Then she wondered where that had come from. Something buzzed around her, and her vision blurred for a moment. She brushed it away. When she placed her foot down, a feeling of lassitude enveloped her. Hugh motioned for her to come closer, holding out another chair, but she couldn't move. Her feet felt glued to the floor.

* * *

Eli watched the younger man, his face grim. He rarely left the house, but he sensed Remy had to be watched. She was as fragile as the lace on her dresser, yet she insisted on acting brave. Captain Eli Gaspar would bet the last of his pipe tobacco that the man had more than tea on his mind, and someone had to keep an eye on the girl. After all, as a member of his crew, she became his responsibility.

* * *

Hugh's phone rang. "Ah, here we go." He listened intently, his face serious, his gray eyes watching her. "I see. No, she's right here. I'll let her know. When can she reopen?"

He slid the phone into his back pocket.

"Well?" she asked from her spot, forcing her legs to move closer. Taking a deep breath, she shook off the feeling of restraint, the graciousness in Hugh's eyes more inviting than the hesitation she knew ravaged her soul.

"It was definitely arson. They feel strongly it was mischief, and they're betting on kids. It made a mess but didn't cause any real harm. Do you have any enemies?"

"No, not at all." She thought briefly about the break-in at her house. Her eyes clouded over.

Hugh moved closer. "What are you thinking about? Are you worried? It's just a small scorch mark that you'll be able to buff right out."

"There wasn't much damage," Remy agreed. "Well, I better go."

Hugh stayed her with his hand. "Detective Saunders asked for you to wait. He'll be here soon." He smiled and said, "Would you like the nickel tour?"

"What if I don't have a nickel?" Remy asked playfully. She liked Hugh. They were closer now. The room was hushed as well, like a church. Remy smiled at that. It was as though the world narrowed to the two of them. "In for a nickel, in for a pound," she thought with a laugh. She might as well. She nodded. After all, the police had asked her to wait there.

He pulled a coin from his tight jeans and placed it on the mahogany desk. "My treat." He held out a hand to invite her to the first display. She hesitated, but he reached for her. Raising her own small hand, she placed it in his warm clasp, and a feeling of rightness overwhelmed her. They looked at each other. A sigh escaped her lips as Hugh's hand encased her own.

They walked over to the first display, seeing the artifacts, but each one's mind and body buzzed with the awareness of the other. Remy squirmed with the onslaught of emotions. She could feel her hormones move into overdrive. She watched his lips as he talked and wondered what he would think of her if she threw him down on the ratty rug to have her wicked way with him. If she could remember a wicked way, she would surely have it, she knew with certainty.

He was talking about telescopes, so she forced her eyes to rest on the shiny brass, seeing only Hugh, and his broad shoulders narrowing to a tight—

"It was always a popular hamlet," Hugh told her, his face alight with humor, his voice serious.

A lighted case had commemorative telescopes, a naval saber from the Civil War, dress gloves, and a ship's log. Remy strolled past, not particularly interested, but she listened politely to Hugh as he explained each display. There were framed yellow maps and newspapers describing the changing town.

"Hamlet?" she asked, showing she was a good listener. "Not," she thought.

"Small town." Hugh pointed to an old map. "Glaciers carved out our harbor about twenty thousand years ago. They left behind all those big boulders dotting the hills. We have a natural harbor."

"What does that mean?" Remy asked, warming to his enthusiasm. He talked lovingly of his little museum, his arms working to point out this and that. Remy watched the enjoyment in his face, lost in the deep resonance of his voice. Her mother's words from a few days ago echoed in her head. "Once you know, you just know." She searched her memory from the beginning with Scott. He was fun. She enjoyed him, but there was not the gut-punching sense of...what? What was she feeling? She forced herself to pay attention to him. Was it lust? Could desire have been doing this?

Surely coupled with loneliness, the need to interact with a man was strong, but this was something else. She had male students whom she worked with daily. She never saw them as anything more than bodies that needed to be stretched to their capacities for exercise. Licking her lips, she wondered if his pecs were dusted with hair or smooth. Oh, he would never be interested in someone like her. He was smart, worldly, knew about this kind of stuff. All she knew about was yoga and what kind of mayo to put on a sandwich.

Hugh smiled. "It means that ships can sail right into the harbor and dock here. That makes it easy to get cargo on and off the ships. That's very important." He took her to a large chest of drawers, polished to within an inch of its life. She saw that it belonged to a famous family in the area. "This is all significant." He moved his hand expansively. "It shows that furniture was made here. This was no backwater. It was an important place."

The tour felt intimate, his voice hushed, reverent. *"It's hard to believe we're talking about fish."* Remy didn't realize she'd said it aloud.

"No, no. They're mammals. They breastfeed."

"We are talking about whales?" Remy asked quietly.

They came upon a diorama of a Native American village. "We weren't the first settlers in the—"

"We?" she questioned, raising an arched brow. She was aiming to concentrate better. She didn't want to make a fool of herself. Squashing her attraction, she focused on his tour.

"We, as in my father's family. They are longtime residents of the area. Anyway, getting back to the subject, we weren't the first settlers here. The Matinecocks first settled here thousands of years ago. They sold the land to the English for a collection of hatchets and knives, some shirts, nails, and needles."

"Not a great deal for the Matinecocks," Remy said.

"I'm not very proud of it," Hugh said. "But that was the way of it." They stared at the collection of shells and arrowheads. He picked one out of the display, toying with the sharp point against the pad of his thumb. For a minute, he seemed lost in thought, as if he were debating something, then he blurted, "They're mine." He was embarrassed.

"He's a nerd," Remy thought. Happiness overwhelmed her. It didn't bother her. "Me too," she wanted to shout.

"I dug most of these up on my parents' property. Not something I like to admit on a first date."

"Is this a date?" Remy asked, her tone teasing, the dimple in her cheek showing. She liked the way he looked at her, his gray eyes caressing her face.

He tucked the arrowhead carefully in the case. "I'm sure you've been on worse."

She turned to look him full in the face. It wasn't fair to have such a handsome mayor. He probably fought off his constituents. "Who says this is bad?" she asked softly.

The lights flickered, breaking the mood.

Hugh directed her to the next case. "The area grew, becoming famous for its mills. These two men." They walked over to two portraits flanking the back walls of the church. They sat stiffly, looking out at the world grimly. "These are the Jones Brothers. They put Cold Spring, as it was known in those days, on the map. My ancestor… oh…I think it's finally warming up in here."

Remy agreed. Her nose had feeling again. It was decidedly warmer in the room. In fact, she felt too warm in her clothes. She took off her jacket, and Hugh hung it on a rolling chair. She studied the serious faces above her.

"They bought a fleet of whaling ships in the mid-nineteenth century, making Cold Spring rival the great whaling harbors of Massachusetts."

"What's up with all this?" She gestured to the collection of carved scrimshaw in a glass case.

Hugh blushed and shrugged. "I like whales. I just do. I think they are majestic, beautiful. Did you ever see one in the wild?"

Remy shook her head that she hadn't, caught up in his energy.

"The whalers and the whaling industry decimated the population, killed thousands of whales."

"So, why would you venerate the whole thing?"

"Someone's got to remember it. Interactive museums, little displays like this remind people of what we are capable of doing. If it's not recorded or studied, we're bound to repeat it. I feel like it's some sort of restitution. My seventh great-grandfather was a whaler. That's where I got my first scrimshaw."

Remy wiped the sheen of perspiration from her forehead. The pipes clanged loudly, startling both Hugh and Remy. He walked over to check the thermostat.

"Humph. Damnedest thing." He flicked it with his finger.

Hugh fiddled with the knob, then walked over to the table case filled with various tools made from whalebone. "Some animal gave its life for these trinkets."

Remy joined him. Hugh opened it, taking out a device with a carved handle attached to a scalloped disk. It had yellowed with age. Hugh placed it in her hands. Remy looked at him with a question in her eyes.

"It's a pie crust trimmer."

Remy smiled, running her finger on the delicate rim of the disc. "What are these?" She gestured to a row on flat sticks next to a group of etched whale's teeth.

"Busks." Hugh took out a flat, narrow whalebone shaped like an emery board.

"I can't imagine—"

"It's a very personal item." Hugh's voice dropped, and he moved closer. Remy couldn't stop staring at those lips. "Men made them for their sweethearts to wear in their corsets as a reminder while the men were away."

"Did your seventh great-grandfather make one of these?" she asked in a husky whisper.

"I can't believe I'm flirting over fossils," Remy thought, swaying closer. Hugh handed the smooth whalebone to Remy. Her fingers touched the carved words reverently.

Remy placed it across her breast, over her heart. The air stilled, and Hugh leaned forward. "He's going to kiss me," she thought dreamily. Her eyes slid shut, and she felt him lean into her, his lips lightly grazing hers. The register book fell heavily to the floor, causing them to jump. They parted guiltily. It lay splayed, the pages rifling as though a breeze blew over them.

She blinked up at Hugh and handed him the busk. "It couldn't have been comfortable, do you think?"

Hugh cleared his throat. "Maybe it wasn't supposed to be." There was another pregnant pause, and Remy's eyes were drawn to a portrait near the door.

Remy nodded, her gaze caught on the face of a beautiful woman with a blond chignon, who smiled down at her. "Who is this?" She walked over to the painting.

"That's Sarah—" Hugh said, but he was interrupted by the detective's arrival.

Detective Saunders was a tall man, a former highway patrolman, now a plainclothes officer, who walked purposefully toward the couple. He had a head of ginger hair and the milky skin of a redhead. He smiled politely at Remy.

"As I told the mayor, however amateurish, it was definitely arson. Can you think of anyone who would do this to you?"

Remy shook her head. Hugh touched her back in a comforting way, and with surprise, Remy chose not to move away. His large hand felt good against the thin material of her shirt. He rested his hand comfortingly on her shoulder.

"Well, keep an eye out for anything suspicious. We'll send an extra patrol car to circle past your home later tonight."

"I can have my class at four?"

Saunders nodded. "We're done in there. Call Jacar's Hardware. They'll board up the window."

The detective nodded to Hugh grimly, then left the museum.

Remy turned to Hugh and grinned. "Thanks for the tour."

"You didn't get your nickel's worth. Did I bore you terribly?" He smiled, moving closer to her. He brushed the hair from her face. Time stood still. The bell over the door tinkled in the silence, and the mood changed.

"No, not at all," she said, meaning it. "I'll come back with my daughter, Olivia. She'll enjoy looking at the whale teeth."

"Scrimshaw." They both glanced back at the table filled with its collection of whale ivory painstakingly carved or etched with colorful scenes. "It really is fascinating. Did you inherit all of these?" Remy liked the way his face lit up.

"Only a few. The really bad ones." He picked up a beautifully carved tooth filled with images of brave whalers chasing a huge beast.

"Why don't you come for dinner at my house tomorrow," Remy asked him impulsively. Hugh's face brightened.

They exchanged numbers, setting up a time for the next day.

Remy left the church, feeling lighthearted, until she came upon the shattered glass on the walkway to her studio. Grabbing a broom, she swept it up, the bitter cold stinging her cheeks. She arranged for the window to be boarded and fought the feeling of uneasiness. It had to be kids, she convinced herself.

* * *

Hugh sat at his antique desk, a satisfied smile on those sculpted lips. He liked her—really liked her. Remy was hurting. He remembered the feeling, a tightness in his chest blossoming into a protective anger as he watched her struggle with her emotions. She was sweet and adorable. He had met her mother, Judith, recently. She'd become involved in his museum and was just elected co-chair for his charity for children's cancers. Judith had pressed for him to meet her daughter, but he avoided it, eventually going just to fulfill his obligation. What was wrong with Remy's ex? He felt all wired up when he was next to her and had to fight the feeling of wanting to take her in his embrace and whisper that the first one, that loser, was just practice. He knew from his own broken heart that when it finally heals, like a cracked bone, it mends stronger than before.

He never thought of Lauren anymore with anything but regret that it lasted as long as it did, and that they had continued to hurt each other so deeply. They weren't right for each other, a mismatched set that never should have gotten past the first date. But somehow he felt deeply connected to Remy, as if he knew what was going to erupt from her mouth. Her hurt sizzled in his gut like a high-voltage wire. He wanted to help her but wondered how to start. The kiss was a good place to begin. He smiled. "It was interrupted," he thought with chagrin.

He abruptly set down the pen he was holding. The bell. He glanced at the tiny brass object over the front door. It had chimed, stopping his seduction, but no one had come in. He glanced around the empty room, puzzled.

"Henry?" he asked quietly. No one answered.

CHAPTER ELEVEN

Turned out Molly loved yoga. She was slow moving, her thighs weak. She couldn't stop talking, but she enjoyed the class. Since it was just the two of them, Remy allowed her to chatter away as she helped her with beginner's poses. Molly knew everybody in town. She had lived here her entire life, never thinking she'd marry Sal Valenti, the owner of a little antique store on the corner.

"When we met, it was like magic," Molly said, her face animated with happiness. "I had given up, you know. Thought I'd never meet the right guy."

"But you've dated others."

"Yeah," Molly agreed. "I thought…well, I kind of had this thing for my partner."

"Paul Russo?" Remy asked.

"Awkward," she said in a high, singsong voice. "When he lost his wife, I figured that maybe he'd finally see me."

"Did anything happen?"

Molly concentrated on moving into the pigeon pose. Remy got up to readjust her foot. Molly groaned.

"Oh, did I hurt you?" Remy asked.

"No, but I think I may have to spend the rest of the night here. I don't know how I'm going to get up."

Remy laughed. "Don't worry. I'll help you."

"I'm glad I met you. I think sometimes we meet people who become important in our lives, you know, like impact them. I met Paul and thought he was my soul mate. Clearly he wasn't, because he led me to Sal. The office had a professional relationship with him when we hired him to stage homes. It was also because of Paul that I met Georgia. That sure as hell changed my life."

Remy wanted to ask her who Georgia was, but the next class started filing in the door, and the discussion had to be left unfinished.

Molly struggled to her feet, then called out, "By the way, my friend Georgia would love to examine the house you're renting. Can she come by one day?"

Remy was only half-listening, but she nodded. She had to collect the fees for the next group and add two more students to the roster. "Sure," she said absently. "Call me, and we'll arrange it."

Her cell trilled from her desk, and Remy waved goodbye as she answered it. Her mother's voice filled her ear.

"So?"

"Hi, Mom." Remy decided not to share the fire in her studio with her parents. No reason to worry them unnecessarily.

"Did you meet him?"

"Who?" Remy asked.

"Yes. Did you have fun?"

"Mom," Remy hissed. "What are you talking about?"

"Hugh. He told me he was going to visit you today. Did you meet him? Isn't he cute? Did you do anything?"

102

Remy rolled her eyes, pausing for a minute, the happiness in her mother's voice stopping the negative comment from springing from her lips. "Yes," she said simply. "He's very nice."

"I knew you would like him! Brian," she called out. "Remy liked Hugh."

Remy heard her father yell, "Who?"

"Mom, stop. Please stop."

"He's mayor, you know."

"Yes, he told me. Oh, people are filing in, Mom. I have another class."

"All right, honey. I'm just so happy you finally met. I think...I think..." Judith paused.

Time stilled, Remy's breath caught in her throat. Her mother's eagerness infected her spirit, filling it with a buoyancy she hadn't felt since Olivia was born. "Mom?"

"I know there's something special there. Never doubt my intuition, Remy."

"That's a bit premature. Don't get your hopes up."

"I don't know about that, dear. Once you know, you know."

Remy hung up wondering if her mother knew something she didn't.

It was dark by the time Remy finished her last class. She arranged Wednesday to be her late night at the studio, as Olivia spent Wednesdays and alternate weekends with Scott and Prunella. She had a text from Scott earlier and stared at the message miserably. He had a family thing tomorrow night and wanted Olivia to spend Thursday with them as well. She only had to reply if there was a problem. Remy shrugged unhappily. She'd never make things difficult for her daughter and her father. It wasn't in her DNA. She locked the door, scooting to her car, climbing over a small drift of snow. It was filthy outside, the wet snow making for treacherous driving conditions. She had ended class a half hour ago, did her accounting, and cleaned up the studio. One of the women offered to wait, but she insisted they all leave. It was Cold Spring Harbor, after all, she told them. Safest place on earth—until she moved into town, apparently.

It was freezing, the temperature dipping to subzero lows. The town was deserted, and for a minute, Remy shivered from more than the cold breeze coming off the bay. She whipped her head around, feeling as though she were being watched. The wind snatched her breath, and she gasped from the chill. The car was running, the snow a wet pile of slush sliding from the warmed chassis. She had a remote starter, a gift from her parents, so she could start her car from the confines of her home or studio and sit on heated seats. The lights flashed, the door alarm chirped, and she slid into the cozy vehicle.

Remy rubbed her hands together, then put the car into drive to take the short trip home. It was barely two blocks. She couldn't wait for summer, when she would walk home. After she switched on the radio, the music played absently, while she went over her time with Hugh. Pithy remarks came to her, things she could have said to make herself more interesting. But she wasn't interesting, not like him. Somehow the time had passed, and it looked like her lack of small talk didn't affect Hugh. He still seemed eager to see her again. Perhaps she worried too much. Maybe none of it mattered. "When you know, you just know," she thought again, her mother's words echoing in her head.

She pulled onto Main and came to the one light that bisected the town. Christmas lights winked in pretty patterns, outlining the faces of the buildings. She watched the wind send spirals of snow eddying on the blacktop. The car bucked as a gust pushed it, whistling through the crack of the window. It sounded like a deep moan. Remy rested her foot lightly on the brake, wanting to take off as soon as the light changed. When green bathed her face, she took her foot off the brake, ready to accelerate.

Dual headlights filled her rearview mirror. She urged her car forward. The car behind her was sitting practically on top of her rear bumper. "Asshole," she thought. She raised her face and squinted. The bright lights were on. She pressed her pedal, speeding up, feeling a little trapped. The car behind her was traveling a bit too fast. She wanted to get out of its way.

The headlights came up so suddenly. They became large circles in her rear window. Remy bit back a curse, knowing she was going to be hit. Gripping the wheel, her knuckles white under her gloves, she punched the gas and floored the car, feeling the Ford Focus surge forward. She was so intent on getting away, she missed her turn and found herself heading directly toward Route 25A. She made a hard right and noticed the car was a beige sedan. Then she passed Cold Spring Laboratories and the fish hatchery. The other car had barreled straight past her, its horn screaming. It barely missed the tail end of her car.

She went down a quarter mile, slowing to a crawl. Remy made a U-turn into a side street and stopped to catch her breath. Her heart fluttered against the walls of her chest. She reached down, pulling back her purse, which had fallen when she made the quick turn. She searched inside the voluminous bag, and her hand closed around her phone. She placed it in the console between the two seats.

Pulling back onto 25A, she drove cautiously toward Main. She made the left, her eyes opening wide when she saw the headlights coming up again at her fast. The car clipped her hard, throwing her compact forward. The steering wheel slid through her fingers, and her turn became sloppy as she tried to avoid smashing against a stone divider. Remy cursed. She placed both her hands on one side of the steering wheel, making the car swerve sharply. It jerked clumsily, and her head whipped as she spun on black ice.

Using her teeth, she frantically tugged off her gloves, one by one. She fought to steady the wheel, knowing the car was heading for the stone wall that bordered the incline to the inlet.

"Hard port!" She heard a man say from the backseat, of all places. Remy gasped, her startled eyes looked in the rearview mirror. Seeing a bearded man, she screamed, losing total control of the wheel. The other car came up fast and slammed into her right side, sending her into an uncontrolled spin. Her back pressed into the seat as the impact sent her head connecting with the driver's window.

Remy thought she saw a white hand reaching for her, and then she didn't see anything at all.

CHAPTER TWELVE

"**S**he's coming round." Remy heard a relieved voice as if from a tunnel. She was flat on her back on a stretcher, a kaleidoscope of lights flashing around her. The tinny echo of a police radio squawked in the background. Remy attempted to sit up but was pushed back by a strong hand. She raised a shaky hand to her head and touched a bulky bandage.

"How many fingers do you see?"

"Fingers?" She squinted.

"Jeez. Get her to the hospital already," an impatient voice said. "I'll call her folks."

Remy recognized Hugh's voice. "No!" she shouted. "Are you a paramedic too?" she asked in a reedy voice. Was that weak thing her? She cleared her throat.

Hugh took her hand within his warm grasp. "No, they called me because I'm notified of any accidents in the area. You don't want your parents to come?"

"Absolutely not. Wait," she said in a panic as she felt herself lifted. "Where are we going?"

"Hospital," the paramedic offered. "You've got quite the bump there."

"I'm fine. I want to go home. Is my car OK?"

"Well, as long as you have collision, your car is OK."

"Crap." Remy sighed, easing back down, her lips rimmed with white. She felt the stretcher being lifted, and her stomach heaved.

"Do you need a bag?" the paramedic asked professionally.

Remy moaned in response, her stomach dancing around her throat. She was handed a paper bag not unlike what she saw on an airplane.

"You'll feel better in the morning," Hugh said as he hopped into the ambulance.

"You coming, Mayor?"

"Yes," he replied. The doors slammed shut. Remy closed her eyes, fighting the nausea that threatened as the vehicle took off. She was mortified. Her skin must have gone white, because she felt a familiar hand stroke her sweaty forehead. Swallowing thickly, she peered under her lashes, watching Hugh look at her. His concerned gray eyes comforted her. She felt her fingers being squeezed reassuringly.

"You're going to be fine," he whispered.

"Oh, what the hell," Remy thought. If he doesn't mind my tumbleweed hair this afternoon, what's a black eye or two between friends?"

* * *

It was a minor bruise, but they insisted on keeping her for observation. She wouldn't let Hugh call her family, didn't want their sleep interrupted. He offered to pick her up in the morning to drive her home.

Remy must have dozed, because when she opened her eyes, the room swam into focus. She lifted her head, groaning with the heaviness of it. Her face hurt. The skin around her eye sockets was tender. "I must look like a raccoon," Remy thought. Weak light filtered in through the venetian blinds, and the world looked back at her in shades of violet.

A soft snore startled her, and she peered through the gloom and was able to make out the hunched-over figure of a man seated just beyond the nylon curtain. Reaching up, she struggled with the fabric. She winced when the rings holding it squealed loudly. She heard a muffled snort, and a large hand appeared to help her pull back the material. A bleary-eyed Hugh smiled back at her.

"What are you doing here?" she whispered.

"You were a little out of it last night."

"What?" she demanded.

Hugh shrugged sheepishly. "You were crying. Sue me. I can't deal with a weeping female."

"Was it bad?"

"Worse than when the Mets lost the series." He dragged his chair closer to the bed. "How do you feel today?"

Remy touched her head, which was bandaged thickly. "Hurts a bit, but I'll live."

Hugh brightened. "Well, that's a relief."

"Does it look bad?" she asked. "I must look like a mess."

Ever resourceful, Hugh pulled sunglasses from his jacket pocket.

"Do you ever do anything wrong?" Remy asked sourly as she took the glasses and tried them on.

"Nope," he said honestly.

"I'm so sorry. You didn't have to stay," Remy said miserably.

"Why? You asked, and—"

"I asked?" Remy's voice rose.

"More like demanded."

A nurse briskly entered the room, snapping open the blinds, turning jaundiced eyes on Hugh. "You were supposed to leave hours ago, Your Honor."

"I had a meeting about the upcoming lane change," Hugh lied.

"Yeah, sure," the nurse said with raised eyebrows. She looked at her wristwatch. "When, at four in the morning?"

"I was early." He gave her a wide smile that stopped all female breathing in the room. "No wonder you got yourself elected," Remy thought.

Hugh stood and stretched his arms wide. "When is she being released?"

"As soon as the doctor signs. Should be in another hour or so."

Remy held the green hospital gown away from her chest with a thumb and forefinger. Hugh shook his head. "They changed you, I waited outside. Get dressed. I'll take you for breakfast."

He walked out, leaving Remy's folded clothes at the foot of the bed. "Call me if you're dizzy," he said as he left the room.

The ward was just waking up. The nurse stayed to take out Remy's IV. She answered Remy's questions about the hospital. It was a small facility, with a few hundred beds. Mayor Matthews had been good to them. There was talk about closing it down, but he got that squashed right after he was elected. He knew every member of the staff personally just from the holiday fete earlier this year. They raised close to sixty thousand dollars, enough to put in a more modern waiting room, one with a separate play area for children. It was clear that Hugh was loved in the small town.

When Remy came out, Hugh took a small plastic bag from her, and they left, walking side by side to his truck. He asked if she wanted to pick up something to eat or sit in the diner. They chose to eat at her place, so he stopped at a deli and picked up ham and eggs on rolls. With a strange feeling of domesticity, they sat at her kitchen table in the early-morning light.

"What time does Olivia get home?" he asked as he started wrapping up the wax paper from the sandwiches. "Do you have time to lie down? I'll wait for her."

Remy looked at him, her insides melting just a bit. He was so kind. "You barely know me. She doesn't get home until tomorrow anyway."

Hugh blushed. "I can't explain it. I mean, I only went to your studio because your mom was so insistent. It feels like I've known you forever."

Remy nodded in agreement. It did. They seemed to fit together as if they belonged together. "Once you know," Remy thought dreamily.

* * *

Up in the rafters, Marum sighed. Sten looked at her, rolling his eyes. "You're not supposed to be engaged with their feelings."

Marum floated in ecstasy, her hands clasped, her face alight with pleasure. "It's so romantic. Do you think Remy and Hugh are aware that they're kindred spirits?"

Sten stood and brushed off his immaculate iridescent pants, his words designed to bring Marum crashing down to reality.

"Nobody ever knows. I mean, they suspect. They use the term 'soul mates' to death. What do they really know, a feeling of familiarity? They grasp at anything to find that connect, the recognition that brings happiness, then spend the rest of their lives trying to change the other person. Why can't they ever be happy?"

"Were you always so cynical?"

"I'm not a cynic, Marum. I state the obvious."

Marum approached Sten. "You don't think the human heart can recognize its other half?"

"Sure, the astute souls do recognize a kindred, but they won't realize fully until they complete their journey here."

"It's all so stupid," Marum said. "Why can't everything be revealed? The tests, the punishments? It seems cruel."

Sten gave her a warning glance. "What's the point of life then, Marum? We chose our course, then come here to live it with the souls we want to share it with."

"So explain Scott, the creep."

"Stop being judgmental. It's not our job. He is a mere player in the grand scheme. You know that, Marum. We are just here—"

"Yes?" Marum's blue eyes narrowed.

"Consider yourself a traffic cop."

"A traffic cop? Really, Sten. That sounds so pedestrian."

"Marum, they elected you because of your insights. You're here to give a nudge in the right direction. Provide opportunities, insights. You can't make them do what they choose not to. I don't care how many signals you throw in their path, or the many whispers in their dreams, some of them don't listen."

"Because they don't have confidence!" Marum answered hotly.

"You're walking a fine line, sentinel," Sten said sternly. "Confidence is learned. Love is earned. Page nine, paragraph thirty-four. It's in the book. Remy Galway has to make mistakes. They all do. Some change from them, others fail."

Marum sighed loudly again, her face dimming.

"Marum," Sten warned. "Sometimes they are just out of sync. They can't all get what they want. Then nobody would come back."

"What about what they *need?*"

"That sounds suspiciously like a whine, Marum." He pointed a finger at her. "You know the job. Not everybody gets to win."

"Speaking of out of sync, look who's here." Marum gestured to Eli, who was walking around the kitchen table observing the two. "Should we pull him out?"

Sten shook his head. "Not yet. Eli needs them just as much as they need Eli."

"He's not their soul mate."

"No, but you know lost souls are always searching."

"They didn't cover this at sessions," Marum said impatiently. "I still don't understand. If he's out of sync, two kindreds aren't going to help him."

"Maybe you're reading the situation wrong, Marum. Maybe the dynamics are vital to the three of them. Is Eli here to bring Hugh and Remy together, or are Hugh and Remy here to help the captain get home? It's the old chicken and egg thing."

"Oh, so we're back to chickens again." Marum smiled, her humor restored. "You're being rather cryptic," Marum said into the empty space. Sten had vanished.

* * *

Hugh looked over his shoulder, and a chill danced down his spine.

"Are you cold?" he asked.

Remy shook her head. "No, why?"

"It got cold in here. I know a way to warm you up." Hugh smiled, holding out his arms to her. It seemed natural for Remy to step into his embrace. He cleared his throat. "I don't know, it feels like…"

"It feels like I've come home," Remy told him, her voice soft and low.

* * *

Eli circled the two humans, wondering what exactly was going on. He leaned close to the male, sensing the attraction to Remy.

"Wait a minute," he thought, his eyes narrowing with concern. She was pretty banged up, as if she'd been knocked around in a squall. Eli felt guilty after he trashed her place. He knew he wasn't behaving well, especially after she blamed the Scott guy. He had decided to take her under his wing. She really wasn't a bad sort after all. He had tried to protect her in the car, from the Scott guy, of all people. They were fragile things. While he wasn't too fond of the daughter, this one never gave him much trouble. Just what was this sailor's intentions? He blew a blast of cold air, trying to make him uncomfortable enough to leave. They liked heat, these mortals. Didn't she know it wasn't safe? She needed someone to keep her from harm? A woman needs protection. He vaguely remembered watching out for someone else.

He leaned into the man, feeling him shudder. "Nothing's going to happen on my watch," he whispered pointedly.

"Did you say something?" Hugh asked, batting his hand.

Remy looked up at him sleepily. She stretched, moaning when her muscles protested. "No. Do you mind if I lie down? I'm so tired."

"Call your parents and let them know what happened. Go to sleep. I…" He made a decision. "I don't think you should be alone right now."

"You don't have to stay." Remy kissed his cheek feeling the beginnings of a beard. "You could come back tomorrow when I'm in better shape. You must be tired too. You were at the hospital all last night."

"I have to keep my constituents safe. Don't want you slipping over to the Republican side."

Knowing he wanted to stay made her insides melt. "You don't have to," she whispered huskily.

"I want to."

Remy stood, pulling him close. She reached up to kiss him softly on the lips. "Thanks," she whispered, then shivered, feeling a chill. "You are right, it is getting chilly in here."

Remy went upstairs after alerting her parents about her accident. They wanted to come. She insisted she was fine, told them she was taking a nap. She never mentioned Hugh was staying.

* * *

Hugh entered the den, taking in the dangling arm of the television on the wall. He ran out to pull a small tool kit from the back of his truck and worked in the silence of the house. It had started snowing, and the world was taking on that muted, cozy feel. When he found a woodpile outside, he loaded up a stack next to the hearth, then stirred up a nice fire in the parlor, toasting the room. Hugh paused and dug into the logs. The feeling that he was being watched made him uncomfortable. He crouched by the fire, and his eyes darted around the room.

He spun, the poker raised in his hands, just in time to see the outline of a man against the shadowy walls. He blinked, and the vision was gone, but the mural of the old sea captain pulled him closer. He inched up to it, drawn by the captain's glare. Hugh leaned close, and the captain stared back in a feral snarl. How had he missed that? Why would the painter make such an unfriendly face on the character?

The dark eyes glared back angrily, the bearded face taut with hatred. Hugh's shoulders hunched with the same feeling that he was being watched from the opposite direction. He pivoted, and this time a gray fog wavered. Hugh gasped and rubbed his eyes tiredly. He fell into a winged chair, thinking he must be more exhausted than he realized.

When he opened his eyes, on the edge of his vision, the air moved again. He heard light footsteps on the narrow staircase.

He walked silently up the stairs brandishing a poker.

"Rem," he whispered cautiously. He climbed the steps slowly. Reaching the top, he peered into the half-opened room. Remy lay amid a fluffy white comforter, her head buried in the pillow, her small foot exposed.

* * *

Eli watched Hugh suspiciously as he approached the sleeping woman. While the poker was now down, he didn't trust the young man. Winding up his fist, Eli was poised, ready to attack.

Marum hovered overhead, prepared to interfere with Eli. Sten appeared from thin air. His hand stopped her. "Wait. It will be all right."

They watched raptly as Hugh lifted Remy's foot, tucking it under the plump coverlet. She sighed prettily, her eyes opening, a satisfied smile on her face. Hugh tenderly brushed back the hair from her face.

Eli skidded to a stop. Perhaps he had been too hasty with this human. He debated his next move, leaving it to them to decide for him.

Remy held out her hand. Hugh leaned down and, wrapped her in an embrace. Remy lifted her face to his. Hugh kissed her sweetly, then again, and again.

"I have to stop, or I won't leave," he told her, his cheek leaning against hers. "Go to sleep. I'll watch over you." He glanced around the room warily. "I'll never let anything happen to you."

Eli's face reddened. His skin tightened in embarrassment. He smacked the walls with his fists, creating small torrents of wind. That was what a real man was supposed to do. That is exactly what he didn't do. He didn't protect Henry, his ship, his crew members, his wife, or even his...there was more. He couldn't protect...who else...who else had he failed? He evaporated with shame.

* * *

The house brightened after Hugh closed her door. He sat in the tiny living room, turning the chair away from the sullen captain. Pulling a stack of magazines from the study, he managed to catch up on all the crap of modern culture, from Bieber to the Kardashians. Not that he really cared. But it served as a mild diversion from the face on the wall. Either way, Hugh said to himself, he'd rather look at a serial killer than the scowling captain.

CHAPTER THIRTEEN

Off the coast of Puerto Rico, six days at sea, 1840

H is eyes had swelled shut, glued together from the salt. Not that it mattered. He was sun blind. He could barely make out things close to him. His jacket was gone, his shirt shredded into strips to tie him on to the roof of the afterhouse. It was all that remained of his ship. He had managed to grab some rope and secure the boy to the rocking wood. The roof floated on the water, he and Henry tied to the top. His skin felt like it had shrunk from too many washings. It pulled tightly across his back. The cabin boy still lived, but barely, no thanks to him.

"Henry," he called out, his voice a mere croak. "Henry, speak to me, lad."

The boy moaned, his head rolling on the wooden boards, his fingernails torn and bloody. If Eli didn't get them some water soon, they were as good as dead. Dead as his bloody ship. Dead as his crew.

Eli forced himself to raise his head. He untied his hand, cupping the warm seawater, to dash it across his face. The salty water burned his face as if his skin were flayed. Cursing, he untied his ankles to crawl over to the boy. He nearly cried out from the pain of his burned skin. With shaking hands, he brushed back Henry's matted curls. Henry's cracked lips parted as he cried, his body too depleted to release tears.

"We're dead men, Cap'n. Let me go. Roll me into the water. I'm tired," Henry pleaded.

"No, no, Henry. We'll get saved. I told you the after-house would keep us safe."

Eli looked down at the tourniquet he had created above the child's knee. The wound had stopped bleeding. Maybe he should let the lad slip quietly under the water. What if they did manage to get rescued? What use was a twelve-year-old with one leg? It had snapped like weak kindling when the ship went down. He was near drained of blood by the time Eli reached him. Using his belt, he had tied it off.

He dragged Henry to the center of the makeshift raft, keeping a steady watch for the pesky sharks that circled.

"I'm done for," the boy protested. "Let me go. Please let me go. Even if we get rescued, who will want me now? I'm tired. I'm so tired."

Eli barely slept. He touched the boy's wrist, bound tight to broken timber. Loosening the knot, he glanced down at the pale face. Eli bit his raw knuckle with indecision. Should he let him slide away? Would it matter? He was not God, but a man. A man who promised to bring this boy home to his parents. He retied the rope, binding the boy to the flotsam.

"I made a vow to bring you home. We have to get home to your parents, and I have to go back to my wife and children."

Henry didn't respond. Eli panicked, his fingers probing the boy's face. "Don't leave me, Henry! I promised your mother. I promised Sarah." His hands pulled the boy's head up, the faint breaths assuring Eli the lad still lived. "Don't leave me, boy. I made a promise. Stay with me here. Stay with me in the afterhouse." He kept repeating the words long after he knew Henry couldn't hear him.

CHAPTER FOURTEEN

2014

At eleven, Hugh woke Remy because the police arrived, asking all kinds of questions. They left later, unsatisfied with her responses. All she was able to give them was the fact that it was a beige sedan. Paint from the other car was on her bumper as well. He helped her contact her insurance broker, then drove her over to the rental place. They parted ways reluctantly after she got the keys to her rental car.

"You didn't have to stay. I feel like problems follow me like a shadow. All I am is work." Remy touched his arm.

Hugh shuffled his feet in the cold. "I love work. Truly, I don't mind. You definitely feel better?"

"Good as new. I really enjoyed our time together. I mean, except when I was unconscious."

"Yeah, I enjoyed it too. I'd like to see you again. Especially when you're not unconscious."

"Well," Remy said shyly, "do you want to take a chance being the rebound guy?"

"I'm up for the challenge." Hugh smiled back. "I'll be back later. Try to rest." He paused for a minute, cocking his head. "Remy, do you ever feel things in the house?"

"Like what?"

"Oh, I don't know—like someone's in the house?"

"Why? Did you see something?"

Hugh's face heated. "No, of course not. Maybe the old sea captain's portrait spooked me."

"What, our captain? He may be intense, but I swear sometimes I think he's smiling."

Hugh shivered. "Smiling?" He changed the subject. "I think his name was Elijah something. I'll look him up."

"I'd love to have some information on him. Thanks." Remy reached up to kiss him on the cheek, but Hugh turned, taking her into his arms. She felt warm, secure, and oddly safe. Their bulky parkas separated them, but their bodies locked together magnetically. The kiss deepened, and they found themselves breathing in tandem with each other. Hugh was sweating.

"You have too many clothes on," Remy said.

"My thoughts exactly," Hugh said, kissing her again. "When I'm with you, I feel like I'm…I don't know…like whole."

"I've never done this with anybody," she said.

"I never felt about a woman like—" he said at the same time.

"This is scaring me, Hugh. I want to take it slow." Remy played with the fabric of the Burberry scarf he wore.

Hugh lifted her against him, his smile wide. "Well, I don't. Around here we like to keep traffic moving briskly. Look, Remy. This isn't my first rodeo. I've been married and divorced. I've had a few relationships, but when I saw you, it was like...I don't know...pow!"

Remy rested her head against his chest, listening to the reassuring thud of his heart. "I know, I know. I just don't want to make another mistake. I don't want to get hurt again."

Hugh pulled her face up. "I will never let anything bad happen to you. Ever."

"I'm a package deal, though. Are you prepared for that?"

"Package deal?"

"I come as a plus one, Hugh. I have a little girl."

"A bargain. Two-for-one special. I still wouldn't let anything happen to you. Either of you."

* * *

Eli sat frozen on the awning of the building, a tidal wave of a roar building in his barrel chest. He kicked the canvas with his booted foot, sending a small avalanche of snow onto Remy and Hugh's unsuspecting heads. Remy squealed as they hurried farther down the street to brush off the icy flakes. Eli looked out to the sea, wishing he were in hell. Maybe he was.

CHAPTER FIFTEEN

Her dad was waiting at her door with a golden lab on a leash.

"This here is Scout," he informed his daughter as he led in her new watchdog. He was a giant brute with a sloppy pink tongue that left a trail of drool along her pristine wooden floors.

"Dad!" Remy wailed, looking at the slimy ropes scalloped on the floor.

"Remy!" Brian shouted, seeing her black eyes and bruised cheek. "Why didn't you tell us you were that injured?"

"Take him back, Dad. I don't have the time to take care of a pet."

"Never mind. Let me look at your face."

He held her head tenderly in his large hands, turning it into better light, his face wincing.

"This is bad." He released her. "Scout is here to take care of you," he told her while he unpacked a score of bags filled with dog food and other pet-related products.

"A dog? Like I need this?"

"It's either Mom and me or the dog, Rem. Take your pick."

"You hate dogs. Where'd you get him?" Remy asked, bending to ruffle the yellow fur.

"The pound. They said he was a good watchdog."

For years Remy had begged for a pet, but her parents had steadfastly refused. They were not animal people, her father told her. He was bitten as a child and had a hard time with big dogs. She knew it must have taken a major toll on her father to go to the pound and pick a dog.

"Welcome home, Scout," Remy replied, because she knew that was the end of that.

Brian sat in her parlor, the ever-present newspaper in his hands, Scout at his feet, and a fire roared in the fireplace. Every so often, he bent down to pat the dog awkwardly on the head. Scout slavishly rolled his tongue on her dad's wrist.

"Huh, tickles." He laughed. "Maybe I'll keep your mother away for a while, Rem. She's not going to take your face too well."

"Not a bad idea, Dad." Remy winced as she drank down her tea. "Maybe you should take him home. Looks like you made a friend."

"Never mind, Remy. What did the police say?"

"Since I didn't see a license plate, they don't have much to go on. They found beige paint on my car, and—"

"What color is Scott's car?" He looked at her over the newspaper, his glasses sliding down his big nose.

"Don't go there, Dad. Scott and I may have our differences, but he has no reason to do anything to me."

"He has motive," Brian said as he stood impatiently to pace the room. He stopped in front of the mural, considering the captain's face.

132

"His name, we think, is Elijah," Remy said. "He doesn't know much either." She giggled. "What motives are you talking about? Scott has no motive. We aren't together. You forgave the loan. Other than Livie, we have no cause to interact."

Brian turned, pointing his finger at her. "It's no laughing matter, Remy. First you have a robbery, then they lob a Molotov cocktail at your studio. Who knows what's in Scott's head? He was a fool to leave you." Scout raised his head and barked at his tone.

"Ah, thanks, Dad. How did you know about the vandalism at the studio?"

"You made the six o'clock news," Brian said grimly.

"I was going to tell you about it today," Remy said, her face blushing.

Brian returned a stern look.

"Anyway, it was nothing really. They think it was kids."

Brian harrumphed.

Remy continued as if he hadn't.

"My life with Scott is over. Really over. I'm building a new life. I'm a big girl. You have to let me grow up."

"Then you're run off the road." He went on as if she hadn't spoken. "Why didn't you call us to pick you up from the hospital?"

"Hugh did."

"Who?"

"Oh, this might become a problem. Not who, Hugh."

"The museum fella. How did that happen?"

"It seems he's the mayor, and he was on the scene, so he, well, he sort of watched over me."

Brian grunted, and his eyes narrowed. "What color is his car?"

"Dad," Remy shouted. "He's the mayor."

"I didn't know being a politician exempts a person from crime." Brian grabbed his coat. Remy stood to help him get into it. "I just want you safe, Rem. You're all we have."

"Ditto, Dad. I'm fine. I'm not stupid either. It's just random happenings. Kids, a person with a few drinks. Who would want to hurt me?"

She escorted her father to the door, looked down at Scout, and asked him, "Really, Scout. Who would want to hurt me?"

Scout was busy sniffing the wall underneath the captain's portrait. Whining, he pawed the floor and dug at something. Remy pulled on his collar, afraid he'd scratch her newly polished floors. Scout resisted, and Remy gave up. Her body hurt too much to fight him. She locked the doors, lying down on the sofa and wrapped herself up in her afghan. Her brain was too tired to think.

* * *

Eli kicked ineffectually at the dog, who bared his teeth menacingly. Remy rose, lifting up on her elbow to watch the dog struggling with something. He was growling, his jaws locked tight, fighting with thin air.

She got on her knees and reached out to grasp his collar, but the dog's eyes rolled, and he clenched his teeth. "Maybe this wasn't such a good idea," she reasoned. She and her dad were going to have a little talk tomorrow. The dog pulled at an invisible force, rearing back to bark loudly at the wall.

Eli finally got on his feet and climbed up the wall, kicking at the creature now a part of the menagerie he used to call home. He floated above the animal, watching it go mad trying to reach him. It leaped up, snapping at his backside. The damn beast jumped four feet in the air, its feral snarl vibrating in the small confines of the house. First it was the redecorating, then the imp of Satan moved in, and now Cerberus ruled the roost. It was getting mighty crowded in Eli's home, and he didn't like it at all. Not at all. "Just who was running this ship," he demanded of no one in particular.

"This is war," he thought reluctantly. He didn't mind the woman, but this was all too much. He tried to warn her when the hooligans followed her in the car. He owed her one after making the mess, but they were fast getting even. He wasn't too sure about that big lunk of a man who stayed here while she slept. "She's naive, trusting everybody," he thought indignantly. He didn't sign on for the extra duty, and if she didn't listen to her captain, how could he be responsible for the outcome? He shifted uneasily, worried for her. He hadn't felt like this for a long time. Issues, lots of issues, boiled inside of him. Women brought responsibility. Responsibility brought commitment. Was he committing to this new family when he hadn't fulfilled the responsibility to his own wife?

Things were not smooth sailing. He felt bad, but a captain has to run his ship the way he sees fit. He walked across his deck, pondering his choices. Time to have another chat with his boarder. He had to let her in on his backstory. If they were going to live here together, there had to be rules, and as he was the captain, they were his prerogative.

Eli closed his eyes and concentrated on filling out his form. He puffed out his cheeks, feeling gravity pull his skin into place. Skin glued to bones, which molded, his face feeling the warmth of the fire burning in the grate. The pads of his fingers tingled. His legs settled on the hard wood of the floor, and his knees made their presence known. Air filled his lungs. Eli resisted the urge to cough. His eyes blinked as though he had just awakened.

He stood tall, feeling his broad back stretch. He looked straight down at the woman and asked her, "Just what the devil d'ya think you're doing?"

Remy sat up, her back arched, her feet cramping in shock. She tried to rise, but her breath escaped in a long hiss. Her scream sounded as though her throat were squeezed tight. She couldn't get the sound out. Her head pounded, and her eyes rolled in her head as her world narrowed to a grayish fog. Shadows danced before her eyes. Her arms and legs grew heavy, pulling her down into the fuzzy afghan. Remy collapsed like an unstarched blouse to land in a graceful heap on the sofa, lost to everything in her little world.

Eli cursed loudly and fluently as Scout peed on his stocking leg.

He pushed the animal, but only succeeded in feeling the teeth sink into his leg, holding on as if he were a soupbone. He smacked the stubborn head to no avail.

One bitch attacking him, the other out cold on the couch. This place was heading to hell in a hand basket, that was for sure.

Wiggling free, he scooted to the arm of the couch, watching the woman as she lie there. Well, at least she was breathing. He heard her groan before she started to move around. The dog was seated at the foot of the couch, and its brown eyes followed Eli's every move.

"I'm not going to hurt her, you stupid beast," he told Scout, who listened intently. The dog yawned, then settled down to watch them both.

"I'm not a stupid beast!" Remy choked out. She had recovered somewhat, sitting straight on the couch, holding her distance from the tall stranger levitating before her.

"I wasn't talking to you. I meant the bitch—the dog," Eli explained, his voice softer. No need to put her into another swoon. Where was the backbone he saw in the daughter?

"Am I dreaming?" the woman said.

Woman? Pah! She was little more than a girl. He watched her reach out to touch him. He knew she would feel him. He was not quite solid, but of a nature that you knew something was there. She would feel the cold of him, and if she were as adventurous and brave as her daughter, she would be able to define the shape of his body.

Remy looked at the bearded face, then glanced at the mural, her mouth open in astonishment.

"Aye, it's me, all right. I'm here to have a 'come to Jesus' meeting with you," he told her gravely.

She gulped, her amber eyes filling, then brimming over. "Am I to die, then?" she asked in a small voice, her thoughts only on her daughter. Briefly her mind flitted to Hugh. Was she to miss out on that too.

"Oh, wisht, gel. Why do they always go there? We're going to have a little chat, is all."

Remy gingerly scooted over. She prodded his leg. Her hand felt him, but was able to penetrate the apparition.

"Cold as ice, I am. Cold as death," he advised her, his voice gruff.

"Are you a…?"

"Aye, and you have turned my home upside down, you have. You and the devil's handmaiden."

"Devil's handmaiden?"

"The limb of Satan—that daughter of yours." He stood.

"Livie?" Remy's eyes went round. "My Livie?"

"Aye, your *Liv-ie*. Afraid of nothing, that one is. I had a seaman like that once. I don't want to tell you what happened to him," he said in a grave tone.

Remy shivered involuntarily. The captain shook his finger. "Aye, consider this fair warning."

Scout growled, but Eli was in command once again. Giving the dog a stern look, he nodded in approval when the dog lied down. "Good girl."

"It's a boy. The dog is male."

"I may be dead, but I am not blind. 'Tis female she is. Have you seen her piss? I have." He showed her his wet ankle. "If it were a he, he would have reached my thigh. Turn her over if you don't believe me."

138

"Oh." Remy's mouth opened, then closed abruptly. She rubbed her eyes. Glancing at the portrait, she looked at Eli, then back to the mural. Placing her hands over her mouth, she stifled a scream.

"Before you start to caterwaul, I'd like to know your stance on chickens."

"Chickens?" Remy's scream was diverted.

"Can't abide by them myself. Make a racket, they do. Run around without their heads." He flitted his fingers in small movements. "Make a fuss. You don't need the mess either."

She had no idea what he was talking about. "Oh my God." Remy inched closer to him. He stood tall; she barely reached his shoulder. As she walked around him, he smiled back at her, admiring her as well.

"You're a fine piece yourself, my girl, but these shenanigans have got to go."

Remy leaned toward the coffee table, bending slightly to grab her cell. Eli seized her wrist and held her tight in his frigid embrace.

"I can't touch you for long, gel. Your skin will freeze. Think what they'll do with you if you say something. They put old Pat away, and he was deader than a doornail a few weeks later."

Remy stood firm and bit her lips.

"Fancy a stay in a nuthouse?" Eli continued.

Remy released the phone, and just as quickly, Eli let go of her wrist. Remy rubbed the cold skin.

"I don't believe this is happening," she whispered.

"Most don't. You better sit down before you fall down, miss. You got into quite a kerfuffle, you did."

"Wait a second. I heard you." Remy sank onto the couch. "You were in the car. I saw you. What are you doing in my home?"

Eli walked back and forth before her, his hands crossed behind his back.

"Aha, there lies the crux of the matter. Your house? No, no, no. I hardly think so. *My* house. *My* family home. I live here—always have." He bent down low so that they were face-to-face. While he was pale, Remy admitted the portrait did him little justice. He was stunningly handsome. Though his eyes were blue in the picture, now they were black pits filled with swirling clouds in the deep depths.

Scout growled low in her throat, and the captain spun and pointed a long, pale finger at her. "Stop!" he commanded. "Or it's the plank for you!"

"I thought you were whaler, not a pirate."

Remy was sure that if he had blood, he'd be blushing. When he tightened his lips, she knew she had struck a nerve, even if it was dead. Remy stood her full measure, which she had to admit wasn't much. Hands on hips, she stared up at the captain.

"I don't think so, mister. This is my house now." She felt her knees quake with fear, but locked her legs, ready for battle. No one was going to boss her around in her own home. Balling her hands, she held them loosely at her sides.

Eli turned back to the scared girl. Her blanched face looked as angry as a spitting kitten, he thought with amusement. Throwing back his head, he roared with laughter.

"Instead of a chicken, I got stuck with a bantam cock!" He wheezed a few times, lost in the laughter. "I haven't laughed like that in years, gel. Aye, put your weapons away."

Remy looked down at her fisted hands, feeling foolish. She didn't have anything to combat him.

As if reading her thoughts, the captain agreed. "You don't have much. I'm not here to hurt you. But truly 'tis my house. I lived here with my wife and…someone else. I remember a little girl." He was quiet for a minute and added, "And a babe."

Remy sat down again. How was she going to describe this to anyone? "Well, you don't live here now. What's your full name? I want to look it up."

"Eli Gaspar. Captain Eli Gaspar. I don't mean you no harm. I'm a friendly sort. I don't—"

This time Remy broke into chuckles. "Friendly? Oh my God, I don't believe this."

"What's so funny, gel?"

"Do you watch TV in your hauntings?"

"Don't abide with it. Pat never bothered with things like that."

"I'm being haunted by Gaspar the Friendly Ghost."

"I fail to see the humor." His brows darkened, his face settling into a scowl. Remy had a fair idea what kind of captain he was.

"Oh, trust me, this is funny."

Eli shrugged, his attention diverted to an empty corner. Not even the dog noticed whatever was disturbing him. He stalked over, raising his fist angrily. "What is it now, you fiends of hell?"

Well, that didn't sound good. Remy walked up behind his broad back, peeking over his shoulder to see nothing but air.

"Do you mean the dog?"

"Avast! Leave us alone!" He bellowed so loud, Remy covered her ears.

"He's angry," Marum observed drily.

"So what else is new?" Sten spoke without moving his mouth.

"What does he hope to accomplish by doing this?"

"He's got a plan and doesn't want us listening. Just ignore him." Sten stilled himself so that he nearly faded away.

"I see you, I do!" Eli shook his fist filled with fury. "Leave the gel alone."

"As if it's us," Marum said, smoldering.

"Simmer down, Marum," Sten said quietly. "You know you're not to interact. Don't think he doesn't know that as well. He's just showing off."

"What? What do you see?" Remy asked.

Eli turned, his eyes glowing red. Remy back away, frightened. He grabbed her arm, holding her. His grip tightened, but he was looking through her, his face shocked. He touched his head, whispering, "Char… Charlotte? I have to find Charlotte."

Marum reacted, but Sten held up a hand to stop her. "I want to see what he's planning."

"He's not supposed to touch her," Marum said hotly, then added a hasty, "Sir."

"Patience, Marum. You have to learn patience."

Urgently Eli looked into Remy's face. "I remember now. I have to know what happened to my little girl, my wife. You see, I can't find them. I've come home. I have to know. You must help me."

"I don't know what you are talking about." Remy pulled at her imprisoned wrist uselessly. She pounded against his dead hands. A cold lassitude started freezing her movements. Her eyes drooped. She stopped resisting and whispered, "You're hurting me."

Eli released her so quickly, she fell on the green rug.

"Forgive me," he muttered. "I wouldn't hurt you, no, not at all. Maybe your hell-born babe." He held up a hand to halt her. "Aye, avast there, mother lion. I wouldn't harm a strand of her hair. It's just that, you see…" He fell to his knees, wincing a bit when the bad one hit the floor. He touched her forearm with mute appeal, then said, "I can't find them." His voice was small. "I need to find them."

"Marum," Sten ordered. "Stay put."

"Let me throw him a bone. Please, let me help him remember. After all this time, I think he really wants to know, Sten."

"If he wanted to know, he wouldn't be here." Sten observed Eli intently, then nodded curtly. "All right, go ahead, but it can't be obvious." She heard the warning in his voice. Marum bent next to the dog, sliding the newspaper between her paws.

"I don't know how to help you," Remy said, her heart breaking for him.

A pall of despair settled over the room, filling her heart with his anguish. His pain became her pain. She could feel a heaviness in her own chest. "Look, I don't even know if I believe this is really happening."

"There is a woman." Eli went on as if she hadn't spoken. "I need to speak to her. Bring her here. She will tell me what happened to Charlotte and…my boy. I need to know."

"I can't do that. I don't know who you're talking about."

"Find her," he said as he became transparent. Both he and his voice were fading. "Find her. Her name is Georgia. Georgia Oaken."

"Who?" she asked.

Remy blinked, and he was gone. She stared blankly around the room, silent but for the panting of her new protector, Scout.

"Some watchdog you turned out to be. The least you could have done was bite him. Do you believe what just happened, Scout?"

Scout's paws held her father's discarded newspaper. The dog whined, lifting her paw in appeal. Remy looked around the room, seeing nothing.

Reaching over, she slid the paper from the dog's grip. The paper flopped open to a picture of a woman with two-toned hair, white in the front, black in the rear. She had penetrating obsidian eyes that pulled you to her face. In bold letters it spelled out her name.

"Georgia Oaken," she said aloud. She had heard that name, but where? She couldn't place it. She scanned the page. "Author of *Ghost Followers* and television personality appearing at the Cold Spring Library Sunday, 7:00 p.m.

Contact Molly Valenti for tickets." Aha, Molly mentioned a Georgia, she remembered now. That was tomorrow night.

"Why couldn't I have bought a house with Scooby Doo as a roommate instead?"

* * *

"He is crafty!" Marum burst out. "He was playing on her emotions."

"I don't think she was the only one he was toying with," Sten said, observing his associate.

"In a way, he's cheating. Using us."

"Is that what he'd doing, Marum, or is he surviving? We certainly haven't helped him."

"I thought it was forbidden to assist them. It slows their spiritual growth. They're supposed to figure it out by themselves."

"True." Sten nodded his head. "But you have to reward someone for ingenuity. Well, fledgling, what do you want to do?"

"You're asking me?" Marum said, her iridescent eyes wide with joy. "You're really asking me?"

"They were very happy with your work with Tessa and Gerald. Hemmings House resolved itself very well. I have been given word to let you run the show from here on in. Go ahead, run the show." Sten smiled, and the entire room filled with bright light. "They're growing, you know. Every day. It is thrilling to watch." He pointed to her back.

Marum turned her head to look at her back. Sure enough, the wings were bigger. Not as big as Sten's but certainly noticeable by now.

"Go ahead, flex them," Sten urged. "Try them out."

Marum bunched her shoulders, feeling them stir. She flapped them a bit, and a smile spread across her luminescent face.

"Sten?"

"Yes, dear," the older sentinel answered absently.

"Do you think they make my ass look big?"

CHAPTER SIXTEEN

The phone rang, jarring the quiet of the house. It was Olivia checking in after school. Yes, she was having fun. No, she didn't start her homework. There was a plaintive note in her child's voice, but Olivia would not reveal what was bothering her. They kissed each other good-night for the rest of the evening, saying the usual silly phone ritual, and Remy hung up with an uneasy feeling about her daughter. She wished Livie were home. She would have been if Scott hadn't asked for the extra night. Remy punched a pillow, angry she'd agreed so easily. Maybe it was better if Olivia weren't at home tonight. If she believed what she was seeing, could she be placing her child in jeopardy with the apparition? What if he tried to hurt her daughter? She sat on the couch, curled in a ball, wondering if the whole episode were a hallucination. She began to doubt everything, the gargoyle of insecurity landing on her slumped shoulders, pressing her inward. Maybe she imagined the glorious feeling with Hugh too. He hadn't called all day. Her parents had called twice. They wanted to bring food. She told them she had eaten. Remy had no appetite. She never lied to them, but she found herself answering their questions with monosyllabic answers. If she revealed what she thought had happened, they would insist she move home. If Scott knew, he'd take Livie away. Really, what had happened? She had dreamed of a ghost, probably the product of her slightly disordered mind. Face in hands, Remy watched the corners, willing the captain to come back. Just to make sure he wasn't a dream. She wondered if her situation looked better if he were real. Her eyes kept returning to the mural, observing the captain, watching for any change to reinforce what had happened.

It was cold outside. She looked through the blinds at the watery afternoon sunlight. Remy walked over to the fireplace to throw a log onto the fire in the hearth. She had burned though half her stash due to the cold. She knew Hugh had replenished, but she was running low again. She went to her back door and slipped on well-worn Uggs and an oversized barn jacket to run through the slush to her woodpile. She slid, landing on her side and feeling the freezing snow penetrate her yoga pants. As she went down, she saw movement from the corner of her eye. Twisting in the wet snow, she saw a silhouette of a man run from the clump of bushes underneath her window toward the front of the house. Remy squinted hard through the gloomy late afternoon, her heart racing in her chest.

Getting on all fours, she sprinted to the house in time to hear his booted feet pounding the cobbles in front of her home. She raced up the stone steps two at a time, then jogged to the front of her house. The empty street yawned before her, the silence thick. She stepped into the middle of the street and looked at the deserted blacktop, a shiver racking her slender body. There was no one there—not even a bird. She wrapped her arms around herself protectively in the ill-fitting jacket as she ran for the door. She was afraid to call the police. What if the alleged intruder were as real as the apparition she conversed with earlier? Maybe she imagined him as well. Remy pulled open the door, then closed and locked it. She slid down to the floor to land in a puddle. Scout welcomed her with a wet snout and wagging tail. The dog hadn't even barked. Not once. What could she say? She wasn't sure of anything anymore. At this point, if she called the police, she had nothing to show.

She crawled to the living room and lay her face against the soft rug in total exhaustion. What if she were losing her mind? She slid out of her pants, throwing them into the corner, and wrapped herself in the warm afghan. She stayed cocooned in the warmth of the blanket for a few minutes, hearing the old schoolhouse clock ticking in the silence. Her own breathing sounded loud in her ears. She must have dozed for a minute, because when she opened her eyes, the sun had disappeared leaving the room in total darkness. Scout lay curled next to her on the green rug.

Remy yawned and stretched like a cat. She forced herself to get up. She put on every light in the house, warily looking around. Padding to the laundry room, she pulled out another pair of pants, put them on, then smoothed out her hair in her reflection in the cabinet. Hollow eyes looked back, her freckles so prominent, they looked like someone had dabbed them on. Her cheekbones looked resculpted, as if all her youth were cut away. The large bruise shaded her face, leaving it only half visible.

She stared hard, losing focus for a minute. The glass wavered like liquid. Remy gasped as two faces took shape. She saw close-cut white hair. Remy's eyes opened wide. What was Sting doing in her living room, and who was the woman with him? They were expressionless, with eyes that looked iridescent. Remy spun, her scream interrupted by the strident call of her cell phone. The air shimmered, as did the room. Remy blinked stupidly and looked around. "Dancing Queen" trilled from her phone. That's what her parents called her, their dancing queen. The ring tone was a family joke. She let the call pull her out of the cascading terror. She ran to grab her phone in the living room and yelled a greeting just a shade too loud.

Harsh breathing came through the receiver. There was a laugh, some guttural cursing.

Remy shouted, "Who is this? What do you want?"

"You think you're safe. Sooner or later I'm going to get you. I saw you last night. Tonight I'm going to finish what I started." There was a cackle of laughter. "Take a deep breath, because this may be your last."

Remy threw the phone down, burying her head against the nubby material of the couch. She pressed a hand against her beating heart and forced herself to take great gulping breaths. There would be a record of the phone call, she realized with relief. She finally had something tangible to show somebody.

Remy stretched to grab the phone. She stared at the display, looking at all incoming calls, but there was nothing there, just Olivia's earlier call. Did she imagine her stalker too?

"Captain?" she called out. "Was that you?" She scrolled her phone again but could find no unidentifiable number. "Was that you screwing with me outside? Was it?" she screamed. Her fingers worked fast, combing through the information. "I'm losing my mind," she sang as a mantra, repeating it as if it alone could save her sanity. She threw the phone at the mural. Her hair was wild. She looked like a crazy woman.

"Breathe, Remy," she admonished herself. "Breathe."

She moved into the downward-facing-dog position, letting the blood rush to her head. She put herself into plank, emptying all her thoughts, then did five sun salutations. Her face hurt, her muscles quivered, and just when she thought she couldn't do another, she forced herself to continue. She slid into a resting pose and allowed her heart to calm. She became one with herself.

She didn't know how long she lie in that position until a rapping intruded. It was insistent, finally breaking into her reverie to drag her away from the peaceful spot she had found. She rose, her hand at her throat, trying to take deep breaths to calm her racing heart. Scout's hackles rose, she barked once. Well, at least she was finally performing her duty. Remy glanced at the portrait, looking for the captain.

"Oh, so now you're quiet. Go scare *them!*" she said in an urgent whisper.

The knocking ceased, then started again. She heard her name being shouted. She knew that voice. A smile spread across her face. Hugh. It was Hugh. She ran to the kitchen to let him in. Remy pulled him in by the jacket, slamming the door quickly behind him. Now Scout barked in a wild frenzy. Hugh looked at the dog sternly, forcibly telling her to sit. Scout sat down obediently.

"I didn't notice you had a dog last night," Hugh said.

Hugh was loaded down with packages. She grabbed one. "I didn't."

"Whoa. Slow down. I'll do it." He put the packages on the counter. "You OK?"

"Is there chicken?" she asked, nervously looking in the bags.

"How did you know? I'm going to make roasted—" He pulled a package of poultry from the bag.

"No, no. Put it back. It's a problem."

"You don't like chicken. Everybody likes chicken."

"The captain hates chicken. Oh, Hugh, you are not going to believe the afternoon I've had."

Hugh bent to pat the dog's head. "Is this the captain? Hello, little guy. He doesn't eat chicken?"

"No, that's Scout. My father brought him, I mean her, today. She's a watchdog." She pulled him by the hand. "Come sit down. I have to talk to you."

"Is everything OK?"

"I'm not sure." She led him to the couch. "This afternoon I saw him." She pointed to the illustration on the wall.

"That's the captain you were talking about. Remy, maybe we should call the doctor."

She held up her phone. "Someone called and threatened me, but first, wait a minute," she said breathlessly. "I thought I saw something outside."

"You went out? Remy, it's so cold." He took her in his arms. "How long ago?"

"I don't know." She ran her hand through her hair, looking miserable. "A few minutes...no, I fell asleep. It was a while ago."

"Well, I didn't see anything. Maybe you dreamed it. You're still shaken up. Let me see your phone. Where's the number?" Hugh took her phone to scroll down. "I don't see anything unidentified. Your last call was your daughter. Do you feel all right, Remy? Should I call someone?" He pulled her to the sofa and sat down next to her.

"I'm fine, Hugh." Remy stood impatiently to pace the room. "I was on the couch. He appeared right here." She touched another spot in front of him. "It was real. I touched him. He was ice-cold. A ghost."

Hugh smiled. "Couldn't be a ghost. They're apparitions. You can't really feel them."

"What are you talking about? I know what I felt. Anyway, you're supposed to tell me there are no such things as ghosts."

Hugh leaned forward, pulled her onto his lap, and kissed her gently on the lips. He brushed the hair back from her face. He paused, as if debating whether to say something.

"I don't tell just anybody. You may think I'm crazy. You see, I have a ghost of my own at the church."

"You believe me?"

"Yes," he answered simply. "I believe you. I'd believe you even if I didn't."

"Wait, that makes no sense."

"I know," Hugh said with a grin. "But somehow it's OK."

"You believe in ghosts too? What do you mean, you have a ghost of your own?"

Hugh shook his head. "Happens to be an ancestor of mine. The whaler I told you about. I call him Peg Leg Henry."

"Peg Leg Henry?"

"Yes. He was one of the two survivors of a whaler rammed by a large whale. He was a cabin boy, lost his leg. His captain saved him."

Remy grabbed his shirt collar, her face urgent. "What was his captain's name?"

"It's so odd, coincidental, almost. I looked it up this afternoon. It was—"

"It was me," the captain said from across the room. Hugh protectively put his arms around Remy. He sized the captain up. Remy stiffened and bit her lip.

"Do you see him?" she whispered urgently.

Remy slid off his lap as he stood. He put her behind him.

"You don't have to whisper. I can hear you plain as day," the captain told her. He faced Hugh. "I'm not going to hurt her. You can't be Henry Falcon's descendant. He died when he was a boy."

Hugh reached out, but the captain evaded his touch. "No, he didn't. He was my paternal grandmother's ancestor." Hugh circled him warily.

"He didn't die after I brought him home? How do you know that?" the captain demanded.

Hugh faced him. "I have his journal. He became a successful shipowner. I have a collection of scrimshaw he worked on."

Eli laughed. "What do you know? Did he improve with the etchings?"

"I carry the first one he made in my pocket for good luck." Hugh pulled out the tooth with the childish illustration on its surface. He held it up to the captain. "After all, he had it on him when your ship got wrecked."

Eli looked at the scrimshaw in Hugh's hand. "Aye, that's his. I don't think it's especially lucky. I thought he died from his injuries. He was as good as gone when I brought him home."

"He lived to a ripe old age. He comes by every year on the anniversary of your wreck. You saved him."

"For what? Life as a cripple. When I delivered him, his parents threw me out. He was half-dead when I left, they told me hopeless." His voice was so sad. "Another whaling bark found us two or three days after our sinking. We were almost done for. Henry was nearly drained of blood. I failed his parents. I returned only half of their son."

"Sure, there were challenges, but let me assure you, Henry died a wealthy and happy man. He had fourteen children who ended up being highly successful. Why are you here?" Hugh asked him.

The captain's dark eyes glistened with tears. "I'm not sure..." His voice trailed off. "I got him home, but where did I go? I had a family, a wife, a girl, and…I don't remember much. I need that woman to help me." He faded into the mural.

"Wow. What woman?" Hugh asked.

"Why aren't you freaking out? Do you talk to ghosts every day?"

Hugh pulled Remy up, smiling. "What's up with the chicken? You never told me. Do you know what woman he is talking about?"

"I haven't the faintest idea. He said a name, but I don't remember. Alabama, or something. Should we tell someone? Should we call the police?"

"Alabama? Oh! Maybe Georgia?" Hugh laughed. "That's going to go over really well. They'll fire me. They'll lock us both up. It's been going on for years, weirdness in this house. As soon as Pat started talking about it, they put him away. Besides," he said as he took her hand to move into the kitchen, "I've never heard of anyone getting hurt by one of them. Georgia is not afraid."

"Who is this Georgia?"

"You haven't seen her show? She's amazing."

"How amazing?" Remy asked, narrowing her eyes.

"Talks-to-the-dead amazing. But now, apparently, so do I. I'm hungry. OK, OK." He held up his hands. "Forget about the chicken."

They ended up with pizza, then wine afterward. Hugh built up a fire. With Remy's small feet in his lap, his fingers massaged her toes, while she groaned in ecstasy. Leaning forward, he pulled her into his arms and kissed her thoroughly. Remy looked around the room.

"Forget him." Hugh kissed her deeply. "He left a while ago."

"I have a three-date rule," Remy told him between kisses.

"What? We've been on three dates."

Remy reared back, her eyes luminous in the firelight. He held up his hand, listing the information.

"I took you to tea, I took you to the hospital, and I took you for a rental car. I will admit you're a cheap date."

Remy hugged him. He smelled delicious. Her body hummed with desire. He leaned into her, letting her feel his arousal. "They hardly count." She kissed him on his lips and felt her soul ignite. "Why do you make me feel this way?"

"Because it feels right." Hugh kissed her back.

"Tell me about your marriage," Remy asked softly, brushing the brown hair from his eyes.

Hugh pulled her close to him and let her rest her head on his chest. "Her family belonged to all the same clubs as my parents. They adored her. I was twenty-eight, and they kept asking me to settle down. She was lovely. It wasn't her fault. I don't even know if it was mine. I just knew it wasn't right." He sighed. "We gave up after the second year. Believe me, it broke my heart to end it. I almost stayed, because I didn't want to hurt her, but we both realized it wasn't working. She's married now to some broker in Boston and has three children. What's your war story?"

"I was young, sheltered, and he was everything I thought I wanted. I never dated much, so I jumped at the chance to be with him. I think I wasn't enough for him. Maybe I didn't try enough."

"Maybe he didn't," Hugh kissed her. "I doubt it was you. You just weren't meant for each other."

"Was there anybody else along the way?"

"A few relationships. I didn't invest much, because I didn't want to waste either their time or my own. Flirtations mostly."

"Is this a flirtation?" Remy asked huskily, her amber eyes searching his.

Hugh lifted her against him, kissing her long and hard. "You have to ask? Remy, I've never felt about anyone like this before."

"Me too," she whispered back. "Once you know…"

Their conversation stopped needing words.

CHAPTER SEVENTEEN

Remy fell asleep encased in Hugh's arms. She was exhausted. What began on the living room sofa ended in her full-sized bed, without the baleful stare of the captain upon them. Hugh lifted an additional blanket to wrap around them. The wind whistled through the eaves, the house creaking under the weight of the new snow, which softened all sound.

Hugh squirmed closer to her, wanting to wake her, but felt she needed the sleep more. He kissed the top of her tousled head. His eyes searched the darkened corners of the room, and he gave a startled yelp when he spied the captain observing him from the armoire. The watchdog wagged her tail happily at the apparition.

"Lecher," Hugh whispered hotly. "How long have you been watching us?"

"Long enough. She's a good girl. I hope you'll do right by her."

"Not that it's any of your business," Hugh said. "Welcome to the twenty-first century, Captain. You've been around long enough to know things have changed."

"Aye," the captain said sadly. "Still, 'tis my ship and my rules, so I say you'll—"

They heard something drop downstairs. Scout rose on all fours, her hackles up, her teeth bared. Hugh sat up alertly, letting Remy's head roll onto the pillow.

"Down, Scout," he ordered softly. Sliding out of bed, he stood in all his naked glory.

He heard a throat clearing behind him. "I'm all for scaring the hooligans, but I think you'll do better with your breeches on."

Hugh slipped on pants. He heard the captain's voice again.

"Ahem, weapons, man. We need a weapon and nary a harpoon in sight." The captain looked around the frilly room with a frown. "Take the bat in the corner." Hugh grabbed the bat, holding it beside him as they left the room, closing the door on both Remy and Scout behind him. The captain walked through the door next to him. "Safety in numbers, seaman."

"I'm not a sailor," Hugh whispered.

The captain ignored him. "Take the fore, I'll take the aft," Eli advised as he winked out of sight.

Hugh hugged the wall as he descended the steps. Snow drifted in from outside through the open door. There were no signs of forced entry. A key chain with some sort of fuzzy toy dangling from it hung from the lock in the door. He tiptoed down the steps toward the kitchen. A wet track of puddles sparkled on the wooden floor.

He heard a loud "Psst," and saw the captain embedded in the wall, pointing to the living room.

Hugh and Remy had left her covers and pillow in a rumbled mess on the couch. He saw a vague outline of a man prodding the pile of bedding.

The intruder whispered, "Remy, is that you?" He reached out a hand to pull back the covers. The captain motioned to Hugh that he was going to go in front of him. Scout had gotten out and her sudden, shrill barking added to the terror startling the stranger, who turned quickly. Hugh realized he had a gun in his hand.

Hugh leaped forward and hit the intruder's hand. The gun went off, and the room was bathed in a white flash. Hugh raised the bat, but the other man deflected the attack and hit Hugh's hand with the pistol. Hugh went numb from wrist to elbow. The bat flew out of his grasp and hit Scout, leaving her dazed. Then it dashed into the mural, chipping the paint in two places.

The two men went down hard, wrapped in a tight hold, each trying to overpower the other. The combatants rolled on the floor, and Hugh grabbed the shoulders of the man above him. He punched the other man's face, but the intruder was wearing a ski mask, and the blow rolled off him. Dark eyes gleamed from twin holes. Hugh pushed on his chin, trying to dislodge the disguise. A fist loomed large before his eyes. Hugh knew he was going to get punched, and it was going to be hard. The blow never came. A large vase cracked against the assailant's head, dazing him.

Hugh's attacker went down with a thump. His head banged hard on the wood, and the gun skittered away on the floor. Remy stood over him, her hands still in the air, her bare legs white in the moonlight. Hugh's shirt billowed about her small form. The men both scrambled to their feet, their arms outstretched as they watched for an opportunity to pounce.

Remy ran to the wall and flipped the light switch. When the lights blinked on, Remy recognized the stranger's build.

"Scott!"

Scott pulled off his headgear. "Did I interrupt something, *princess*?" he asked through clenched teeth. He turned to Hugh. "Better get it all now, because once you put a ring on her finger, she stops."

Hugh lunged, his face contorted with rage. His hands locked on Scott's neck. Scott struggled to rip them off.

Remy looked for her phone. Where was her phone? "How could I lose my phone?" she thought frantically. She dodged between the men, pulling at cushions, throwing them around. The fighters tripped as they danced around them. She sliced her foot on a shard of the vase. She yelped with the pain and limped around the room, leaving a trail of bloody footprints.

"I hope you bleed to death," Scott yelled. "That bitch is indestructible. I tried to poison her, and she ended up thinking it was a stomach flu. I've been sitting outside all day freezing my ass off waiting to get in here."

"What?" Remy screeched. "That was you earlier today?" Then she realized what he'd said a moment earlier. "You tried to poison me?"

Scott went on as if she hadn't spoken, his face livid, spittle flying. "Stupid kid I hired couldn't burn her out. She made more damage on my car when I ran her off the road. She's inhuman, you stupid ass. Get out while you can."

Hugh growled with rage, reaching for the other man, but Scott sucker punched him in the chin. Stars danced before his eyes, Hugh weaved around a bit. Scott was barely winded. A trickle of blood from Remy's blow appeared from Scott's hairline. He brushed it away impatiently.

Clearly Hugh was more of a lover than a fighter. Remy watched him waver from the blows. She searched for another object to throw at her ex-husband.

The captain moved to the other side of the room, materializing with a blaze of light and screaming like a rusty door. Hugh felt his own body break out in a cold sweat.

Scott's eyes opened wide. "Holy shit!"

Hugh noticed the direction of his glance. Two sets of eyes spotted the gun on the other side of the room. They both scrambled for the weapon and grappled for possesion. Scott kicked Hugh in the stomach, then kneed him in the head. Dark spots filled Hugh's vision. He went down, his cheek hitting the cold floor with a nasty thud.

He distinctly heard the captain say, "Dork! You were supposed to use the bat!"

Hazily Hugh wondered what it meant. He was sure his teeth were permanently moved. "There goes twelve years of orthodontic work," he thought fleetingly. He could swear birds were flying around the perimeter of the room. Scout crawled over whimpering, licking Hugh's face furiously, trying to get a reaction.

Scott looked up, and Hugh heard him yell as if from a distance. Remy's ex held the gun pointed at the captain, then turned it on Hugh. His face was white, his eyes wild.

"What kind of crazy house is this, Remy?"

"Scott," Remy pleaded. "Put the gun down. Please, stop. Where is Livie?"

Scott ignored her, breathing heavy through clenched teeth.

"Think what you're doing," she implored him.

He aimed at Hugh, who was trying to push up. "Stay down, Lancelot." His eyes searched the room for the apparition. "That's some weird kind of ménage à trois you got going on. I wouldn't have been so hasty to leave if you were open to it, baby-doll."

Hugh roared, shooting to his feet. Eli smiled as he watched Hugh's clumsy attempt to protect Remy.

"Wisht, lad, you fight like a girl," he thought. The captain took this opportunity to come up behind Scott, shoving him hard. Hugh and Scott hit each other, and Hugh spun around and landed in a quiet heap near Remy. Scott pivoted, firing point-blank at the captain, who was now dripping blood and howling with unearthly rage, his hands outstretched toward Scott.

Scott blinked and reached out but saw his hand go right through the apparition. He shivered from the arctic blast. The dog jumped, its sharp teeth locking on to Scott's hand. Scott shook her off furiously and kicked her hard when she landed. Remy heard an inhuman squeal, but she wasn't sure if it was the captain, the dog, or Scott.

Her ex-husband turned, his face blanched but furious. He pointed the gun directly at Remy. "I've had enough of this already. You have more lives than a cat and more bodyguards than the president!"

"No!" Hugh's fingers searched the floor for the bat. He found it. Raising it, he threw himself in front of Remy, his body jerking in midair when the bullet hit him. The bat fell uselessly to the floor, rolling against the wall with a hollow clang. Remy whimpered, fell to her knees, and dragged Hugh into her arms.

"No, no!"

Scott walked over and raised the gun to finish off Remy.

"Where's my daughter?" Remy cried out.

"Home. Asleep under the watchful eye of Priscilla. You don't have to think about her anymore."

"Why?" Remy asked disbelievingly. "Why, Scott? Why are you doing this?" she sobbed.

"Does it matter now?" he asked, shrugging. "No hard feelings, Remy. It's all about the money. Always money. I have a life insurance policy on you. I need—"

He never finished the sentence. Remy watched wide-eyed as the captain whacked him on the head with the bat.

"Call for help," Eli told her before fading into the darkness, his face lined with exhaustion.

* * *

Remy looked at both men lying on the floor. She struggled to her feet and ran on rubbery legs up the stairs, her breathing harsh in her ears. The phone was buried under their clothes in her bedroom.

Scott lie quietly, while Hugh was starting to stir. With shaking hands, she picked up her afghan and wrapped it around his arm, pressing hard. She called 911 using only her thumb. He tried to raise himself on one elbow, so she gently placed his head in her lap.

"What's a dork?" he asked no one in particular.

She knew she spoke to the operator, but couldn't recall even giving her address. Hugh moved around restlessly, but Remy patted him on his head. Crying incoherently, she tried calling her parents to get Livie, but she didn't remember how to use the phone.

The squad car arrived minutes later. Scott was cuffed to the side of his stretcher, despite being unconscious. Two ambulances arrived, one for the prisoner and one for his honor, the mayor.

Hugh was gently reprimanded by a police officer as he took in the carnage. "We have a sheriff, Hugh. We just needed a mayor. A nice, quiet mayor."

"I have to get Livie," Remy wailed to the officer, who assured her they would retrieve her together.

CHAPTER EIGHTEEN

The officer held out the keys that were hanging from the door lock.

"They're my daughter's keys. Please, I have to get to her." Remy was on the sofa, Hugh next to her on a stretcher, the dog panting peacefully at her feet.

Hugh reached out his hand to her. "Please don't drive. Call your parents."

"How could I have been so stupid?" Remy stared at her phone. "Scott called me from Olivia's phone."

"He called you?" the detective asked. "May I see your phone?" The police had been joined by Nassau's finest, two plainclothes detectives.

"I had a threatening call, but the last number to show was my daughter's. I had spoken with her earlier, so I thought I was imagining things. Please take me to her. Please," she implored.

"A squad car is on the way. We'll be taking Priscilla Langly in for questioning. There's another squad car on the way to take you there."

A paramedic finished bandaging Hugh's shoulder.

"How is he?" Remy asked as the man stood.

"It's just a graze. Man!" Hugh laughed. "I've always wanted to say that."

Remy stood on shaky legs. She bent over. "You could have been killed."

"I didn't think, Remy. When I saw...I don't want to live if you're not here." Hugh looked right at her, his heart filled with the sight of her, safe and whole.

A howl erupted from between the walls, and all movement stopped. The detective, police officer, and paramedic exchanged looks.

"It's the dog," Remy assured them.

"Bad fireplace flue," Hugh said at the same time.

The paramedic and detective looked down at the silent dog, rolling their eyes skeptically.

"OK, Your Honor. Get ready for a little ride." They lifted the stretcher to load him into the ambulance waiting beside the door.

"I have to go get my daughter, Hugh. I will come to the hospital as soon as she's safe at home."

"I don't want you driving. I'll be out by tomorrow."

Remy leaned over and kissed his lips gently. "You're the bravest man I know. I never want to be parted from you."

"Me either," Hugh answered. As the door to the ambulance closed, he felt a whisper by his ear. "A dork is a whale's penis. We didn't know about schmucks back then. Next time you jump into a fray, use a better weapon."

Hugh turned to the medic and asked, "You calling me a schmuck?"

"No, sir. Did you hit your head as well?"

The doors slammed shut.

* * *

Marum had a self-satisfied smile on her shiny lips. "Twofers. Two for the price of one!"

"Don't be so cocky, Marum," Sten said. "Eli still is unresolved. While they do love when kindreds hook up, getting a soul home is the primary mission."

"The only thing holding Eli Gaspar back is Eli Gaspar. Look at them." She beamed. "We didn't even guide them, and they found each other!" Marum batted her full-sized wings in all their glorious beauty.

Sten kept his invisible by his side. He eyed her display impatiently, but Marum ignored him. "They are all like that when they first get them," Sten thought.

"Look, it's urgent we get the captain home. I'm just about out of ideas."

"We've still got Olivia. Wait till she gets home," Marum said with a nod.

CHAPTER NINETEEN

Remy and the detective ended up meeting the other squad car at Scott's home. They waited until Priscilla's mother could get there to take the baby. Olivia was beside herself with worry over her little brother. Once her daughter was safe, Remy's anger abated with her fear, and Remy found herself holding Priscilla's mother's hand, promising to help with the baby. He and Olivia shared the same smile.

When they got home, Livie was delighted with her new housemate, Scout. Remy wondered if they should change her name to something more feminine. They talked about it, but Scout she was, and Scout she remained.

Olivia was finally home, safe in the cottage. Remy took the time to explain what had happened. She didn't like lying, so she told Olivia that Daddy and Priscilla had made some poor choices and would have to take a time-out.

Her daughter stood, worry creasing her furrowed brow. "Mommy, Evan can't be alone."

Remy assured her daughter that baby Evan would be safe. They would make sure he did not miss anything important. He would visit them, and they would keep him company.

Remy lay on the bed, hugging her for a good while longer than normal.

Olivia touched her mother's bruised face with tender, baby hands. "Does it hurt?"

"No, not at all," Remy assured her.

Remy left Olivia warm and drowsy and closed the door with a quiet click.

Olivia snuffled, then turned on her side, her eyes popping open. It wasn't that she saw him. She just knew he was in the room.

"Is everyone in this blasted town psychic?" Eli asked from his spot.

Olivia sat up, causing Eli to scoot up her bookcase.

"I won't hurt you," she told him sadly. "I know it wasn't you."

"Ach, he's a silly man, your pa. He'll have plenty of time to think on all this nonsense." Eli settled comfortably on her nightstand. He toyed with the nail polish. "Tell me, have you seen a little girl?"

"Stella?"

"No, I'm sure her name is not Stella. She answers to…Charlotte." He became thoughtful, his eyes masses of swirling clouds. "There was a small boy. A newborn."

Olivia swung her legs over the side of her bed and thought, then shook her head. "I can hear them sometimes, but I don't see them."

He jumped down eagerly. "Where, dear heart? Where do you hear them?"

Olivia pursed her lips. "I have to think." She moved over to her dollhouse standing in the corner. Her grandmother had just bought it when they moved into the house. "Sit here." She patted the raspberry carpet. "Come closer." Her finger touched her lips. "You have to be very quiet."

Eli gingerly sat down next to the girl. "If you find them, I'll never call you a hell-born babe—"

"Shhhh." She closed her bright amber eyes. "Listen."

It was so quiet in the room, Eli found his leg shaking as it used to do when he was impatient. He felt a gentle caress. The girl's touch gave him a weird sort of peace. He rested his back against the wall, listening hard. It started with a faint rustling, then footsteps. Cocking his head, he quieted himself and shut out the groans and whispers that circulated throughout the house.

A reedy song floated on the air. He heard Olivia's quick intake of breath, saw her alert eyes filled with wonder. She pointed to the empty space to the side of them, a smile playing around her upturned lips.

There was laughter. It started low but built up. Eli heard children's voices. They were singing. Chills ran down his spine. He crouched and pressed his ear to a wall that existed to no one but him. He heard a baby cry.

"Thomas." Tears tracked down his face as the memory of his son's name came back with the gale force of a typhoon. The sounds of happiness floated on the ether. His heart seemed to melt in his chest.

Olivia turned her face to him. "Do you hear it?" she asked urgently. Pointing to where the singing was coming from, she told him, "Go to them."

"I can't." He pressed his shoulder against a wall that wouldn't budge. Olivia looked at the spot and shrugged.

"Just step over," she told him. "There's nothing there."

Sweat broke out on Eli's forehead. He heard a voice, a woman, calling the children to return. A sob caught in his throat at the familiar musical sound. It floated down to him, filling him, making his entire being quake with need. The voice receded, growing fainter.

"No, no, no. Don't leave. Don't leave yet," he howled, all his pain and misery wrapped in that sound. "Sarah," he cried. "Sarah, I came home, but you were gone. Where did you take them? I searched for you. I searched for all of you."

There was only the echo of silence. "Sarah, don't leave me." He slid down, powerless against the wall separating him from his loved ones. He landed on the floor in a dejected heap.

Ever practical, Olivia said, "Perhaps you should try the police? They can be very helpful."

Eli lie in a puddle of depression on the floor.

"Mister, Captain, you need to ask for help. When I can't do something, I ask my mommy for help. Don't you have anyone to ask?"

Eli shook his head sadly. "They're all gone. I have no one left."

"Everyone has someone. Even if they don't know it, like my brother, Evan."

Eli crawled into a sitting position. "I *had* somebody. But I was stupid and selfish and thought they would always be there. I didn't care about what was important to them, and because of that, I lost them all." Tears ran from his eyes.

Olivia nodded sagely. "Yes, it's about those choices again."

How did he ever think she was a terror?

"Like my dad. Mommy explained he made some poor choices."

Eli almost laughed, but she was so adorably serious.

"Daddy and Priscilla are going away for a little while. Evan could be alone. But he won't be. He'll have me and my mommy. He won't even realize he's alone, I mean, without his mommy. Everybody has somebody. You just have to let them be with you." Olivia was thoughtful for a minute. "Maybe you could go to the church and talk to the rector. He's very nice."

"Oh, I can just picture that," he said with a little laugh. "Anyway, it's not a church anymore. That Hugh fella turned it into a shrine to whaling." Eli tapped his lips thoughtfully.

Olivia looked up, and he was gone.

CHAPTER TWENTY

It was darker than a tomb, and the snow covered the leaded glass, so that the church was filled with violet shadows. Eli entered tentatively, walking slowly down the aisles, his booted feet making no sound. The wind whistled through the eaves, leaving him unsettled. He glanced warily around, peering closely, his mouth moving as he read each display. There was a model of his ship—recreated from what, he could only guess—and also, in the artificially colored water, a giant sperm whale, caught in the ropes from the deadly harpoons. Whaleboats hung permanently on the frozen waves, and colorfully dressed sailors worked the lines.

His finger touched the mighty head of the embattled whale. Eli marveled at its majesty, the grace of its movements, the bigness of one of God's creatures.

He whispered an apology. "We needed the oil. I didn't understand about loss, you poor beast."

Light shone on the scrimshaw display, and the whalebone gleamed in the muted moonlight.

He was drawn to the case. Reaching in, he touched a busk. His fingers found the familiar grooves and lettering.

Picking it up, he placed it against his lips, knowing the words, because they were scored on his heart.

"And the two shall become one flesh," he whispered softly, tears prickling his eyes. He looked up and saw her beloved face frozen in a painted portrait. His chest tightened, and a sob escaped, as he cried, "Sarah."

CHAPTER TWENTY ONE

Cold Spring Harbor, 1841

"**W**ill you be taking the commission, or not, Eli? I can't hold the post forever."

"It's been barely a week since I'm back." Eli looked bleakly out of the plush offices of the Jones Brothers. Walter Jones stood facing the harbor. His brother John sat behind a large mahogany desk.

"Abel Thompson's been chomping at the bit for this bark," Walter told him.

"I'll not have him," John said with a shake of his graying head.

"I lost my last ship," Eli said bleakly. "I lost everything."

"Not everything. You brought Falcon's boy back. Some would call you a hero."

Eli shrugged. "The doctors don't have much hope for him. He's barely alive. I'm no hero." He shook his head.

"You have to move on with your life, Eli. What else can you do?"

Eli considered the bustling harbor in the distance. There was no reason not to take the job. With a shrug he replied, "Aye, I'll take it." He placed his hat on his head to leave. "I'll be ready to ship out in a fortnight."

"Very good then." Walter held out a hand.

Eli walked out into the late May sunshine. The crushed white shells in the street shone brightly. Horses and carriages lined Main Street. Coopers, chandlers, and taverns had all opened, enjoying the rich boom resulting from the Joneses' whaling trade. It was crowded and noisy. Immigrants were joining the population, and houses were going up all along Spring Street. Eli looked out into the harbor. The bobbing mast of his new ship beckoned him. But his heart failed to find joy in the sea. The thought of shipping out left him flat. There was nothing to come home to.

Turning up his street, he walked toward his small white cottage. Gertie was outside, her pale blond hair plastered to her head. She was doing the wash. There was precious little of it for her to do anymore. She looked up, her face wet with perspiration, elbows deep in suds.

"I've a roast prepared for your dinner, sir."

"I'm not hungry," he told her flatly.

"You're wasting away, you are, sir." She clicked her tongue, then went back to her work.

Eli walked up the small hill toward the rose garden. Sarah had arranged the plants so that they bloomed in different colors, waving a welcome to the incoming ships. He climbed the stone steps and entered the cold confines of the house.

They were gone—taken by the cholera weeks before he came home. Gertie was the sole survivor. He cried over the bare beds, the mattresses and linens burned in his own backyard. It came with the immigrants, the burgeoning population. The small town was unprepared for the epic growth. With horse manure in the streets, sanitation became a problem. It began in the spring, and soon half the population was affected. By winter it stole into his home, robbing him, leaving him more destitute than he could have imagined.

His son, Thomas, was first. Little Charlotte died in her mother's embrace. Sarah was too sick to take care of them. They told him Sarah turned to the wall and closed her eyes. The whisper of his name was her last exhale. She died alone, without him. Knowing this ripped out his heart and soul, leaving him an empty shell. He recalled many of their arguments, his impatience, her complaints. She was afraid he would leave her alone with the children and the burden of bringing them up without a father. He didn't respect her needs. He risked his life selfishly, without considering the outcome for her. She feared his death, the thought of their separation, leaving her alone to face an endless dry desert of life without him.

He hadn't thought of her feelings. He believed he needed to provide her with the vanities rather than the real necessities of life. She didn't require the big house or the fancy clothes. In all fairness, she never asked for it. She wanted him to share the joys of their time together. He had heard the term often enough to have remembered it. She was his soul mate, his heart's desire. He burned for her, yet he had squandered his time with her—for what? Trinkets. Status.

Gertie handed him the busk. "She died with your name on her lips, sir."

His fingers glided over the whalebone. They were no longer one flesh. He was alone. Just as his family suffered, then died alone, so he was to end his days as well. A life sentence with no possibility of parole.

After the whale attack, he had been saved by the afterhouse from his own ship. He had floated on it for three days, with young Henry Falcon, and they were rescued by another bark. It had brought him back to the safety of his town, the security of his own little cottage by the sea, Sarah's afterhouse. It was supposed to keep his family safe. Instead, it served as their tomb.

He left the busk, as well as the rest of his belongings, in the house. Walking out to the sea, he looked at the tall masts. He couldn't do it anymore. What was the point of leaving, when he had nothing to come home to. The colorful banner of roses that his wife planted as his welcome reminded him only of the hollow house, devoid of the warmth of love. He just couldn't go on. There was no afterhouse to save him in the murky waters of the bay. He had failed his family, failed his wife, failed his own heart. He couldn't face life without her or the children. He couldn't face her disappointment in eternity either. The calm waters beckoned. He looked back at the cottage on the hill, knowing with all certainty that an afterhouse was an illusion. The water closed over his head, he embraced it, letting it fill his lungs. The light muted, he became weightless, his heavy heart dragged him deeper into the murky depths of oblivion. He knew with certainty that without the ones he loved, there was no safe place. Without the ones he loved, life was meaningless.

* * *

"Walter Jones was furious with you, he had to delay his ships departure for at least a month," a voice told him, pulling him into the present.

Eli spun, and the busk dropped from his hands with a clatter. He heard the thud of a wooden leg as it crossed the floor.

"Jeez, but you scared the shite out of me," Eli muttered, looking at a familiar face.

Old Henry Falcon thought that was just about the funniest thing he'd ever heard.

"You were a mess when they fished you out," Henry said. "Scully found you four or five days later. It was bad. The fish got to you." He shuddered. "I ended up working with the Joneses' whalers. You did miss some good times, Eli. Saved up enough for two ships of my own."

Eli looked at the other man's peg leg.

"Aye," said Henry. "Was a problem on the dance floor, but I married Florence McGowan, and it never interfered in the process of making a passel of children. Thank you for saving me."

Eli bent his head. "You didn't think I was doing you a big favor at the time."

"True, but what do we know?"

"It was such a waste." Eli shook his head.

"No such thing, Captain. We come, we learn, we love, we live—"

"And then we die. What is it all for?"

"You haven't forgiven yourself?" Henry asked.

"How can I? Sarah died alone. I ran off, leaving her to face this horror without me."

"None of us are alone, Eli," Henry said. "You just don't see her."

CHAPTER TWENTY TWO

2014

Eli felt a pull. It started with a gentle tug, sucking him back to the cottage. He wanted to stay and stare up at the portrait of his wife, but the force propelled him over the treetops, toward his little house on the bay.

There was a crowd in the house. Daylight streamed in through the windows. A woman walked with a dish of leaves burning in her hand. The smell enveloped him, made him sleepy, and dragged him into the living room, where he saw Remy leaning on Hugh on the sofa. Little Olivia looked up and right at him when he tumbled into the room.

"You see him!" the woman screeched.

"She's got a voice that could wake the dead. In fact, she just did," Eli thought as he got to his feet.

"I know you can see him too." She pinched Olivia's cheek. "You're gifted."

"How come we can't see him now?" Hugh demanded. He was pale, but his eyes shone bright. His arm was around Remy. They looked so right together.

"He don't want to be seen, that's why," she responded with a smile. She was short, with two-toned hair, a stocky build, and a warm and friendly face. "Some say the sage gets rid of them. I think it just gets rid of the unwanted spirits. Hmm." She wandered over to a corner and concentrated very hard. She motioned for Olivia to take the smoking sage from her hand, then turned to the wall, her brow scrunched together.

"Honey," she said to Olivia. "Do you feel anything different here?"

Olivia shook her head. She didn't.

***

Marum stepped forward, reaching out to touch Georgia.

"Stop, Marum," Sten said. "If you touch her, there's no going back."

"I've thought a long time about this. Eli's failure is our failure too." Marum looked at him with anguish in her luminous eyes. "The only way she'll be able to convince him is if she's touched by one of us. Besides, I like her."

"She'll be changed forever."

"Not necessarily a bad thing. I think she deserves it. Her open mind has helped so many. It's time for her to use more than she's used to."

"If you insist." Sten was giving her a second chance to change her mind.

"I insist," Marum said with a nod. She stepped forward and caressed Georgia's cheek, then shoulder.

Georgia's skin tingled, then turned golden.

Remy sat up, rapt, watching as a spangle of stardust encased the woman Hugh had brought over. She lived in the area, Hugh had explained, and had communicated with some of the livelier ghosts in the old mansions in the area. She now took on an unearthly glow. Startled, Georgia turned in a circle slowly. She covered the spot on her cheek with her hand. A conduit opened, and joy filled her face.

"Oh, I didn't know before," she said to Marum. "You've been here with us all along."

"Who's she talking to now?" Hugh asked, forcing himself to sit up. His arm pained him and he winced. No one answered him.

"Throughout eternity," Marum whispered back.

"I wasn't sure," Georgia said with awe.

"Yes, you were. You've gone to the next level of consciousness. It's time for Eli to go home. If you can do that, there will be no limits for you."

✳ ✳ ✳

Eli stood crankily, complaining that he wished they would stop talking about him as if he weren't there. Georgia turned, her face drained of expression, her voice changing. Olivia ran to her mother and leaned on her leg.

"What happened to her, Mommy?"

"I don't know. Hugh?'

"I've never seen her do this before. Georgia, are you OK?"

Her voice was different.

"Eli," she called out. "Eli, are you done with your adventures?" It was Sarah.

Eli came over to her and dropped to his knees, hiding his face in the pleats of her long skirts. He felt fingers touch his hair. "I failed you." He cried hot tears.

"No, you didn't."

"I left you. I loved you, and I left you. You needed me, you begged for me to stay, but I ignored you. I told you it was all for you."

"Yes, Eli." The hand stroked his hair back from his cold forehead. "What did you find out? Look at me and tell me what you now know."

"I can't, Sarah. I can't. I lied. It wasn't for you. It was for me. All I cared about was the fun of it, the chase. I admired how I looked providing you with nice things. I thought I loved you, but I didn't understand what love meant."

"What does it mean?"

"If I loved you, I shouldn't have left you." He bent over, and his form was wracked with sobs.

"What's going on?" Remy whispered. All she saw was Georgia deep in a trance, her face devoid of expression.

"I don't know, but I don't want to disturb her." Hugh watched her intently. "What I want to know is, where's Eli? Do you hear anything?"

Remy shook her head. She turned to her daughter. "Livie?"

Olivia put her finger before her lips, indicating for them to be quiet.

Sarah went down on her knees. Her arms surrounded Eli.

"I knew you loved me and the children, Eli." She pushed up his chin. "Love is more than that. Love is knowing that someone else's happiness is more important than your own. Love is knowing how to make the right choices. Do you think if I wanted you to stay, you wouldn't have? It would have made you miserable. More than anything, I wanted your happiness too."

"You forgive me?" Eli asked, hope in his eyes.

"No." Sarah took his hand. "I never had to forgive you. I was never angry at you. You have to forgive yourself. Come home with me, Eli. Your children need you. It's time for you to come home. I think you're finally ready to be with us." She placed his hand on top of her chest. Eli could feel the outline of the busk he had made her so very long ago.

"And the two shall become one flesh," Eli whispered.

"One flesh, one heart, one soul," Sarah said, finishing the line. "It's time for your adventures to end, Eli. It's time for you to come home."

Eli stood and took her hand, "Aye, Sarah mine. 'Tis time for me to meet our son and see my Charlotte. Did her teeth ever come in?" he asked with a smile.

Sarah nodded, as she held out her hand. The air became still, except for a section that grew hazy, then liquid. Eli stepped toward it without a backward glance, to unite his heart to its only mate, to the safety of his own afterhouse. The afterhouse with Sarah.

The room changed. Georgia looked blankly at them.

"It's over. They left." Georgia took a deep breath as she sank to her knees. "That was...wild." She widened her eyes. "I don't want to sound corny, but I think I've been touched by an angel."

"I don't know." Hugh walked over to help her stand. "You put on quite a one-woman show. Where's the captain?"

"Home. He went home."

"Will he come back?" Olivia asked.

"No. He's where he's supposed to be. That was... intense. Thanks for letting me in here. I've always wanted to sage this place, but Pat wouldn't let me. Really, thank you. That was extraordinary."

"I hope he found peace," Remy said. "We kind of owe him."

"Oh, he found peace and forgiveness. Well, I've gotta go. There's a boat in the harbor they want me to investigate. It seems it keeps charting a strange course."

Hugh held up his hand. "Thanks, can't help you there. It's out of my jurisdiction."

Remy escorted her out, then returned to find Hugh alone. "Where's Livie?"

"She's writing a letter to Scott."

Remy started after her.

"Stop, Rem. It was my idea," said Hugh. "I wanted to be alone with you for a minute."

He pulled her close to him and she felt something in the pocket of his pants. "Is that a gun, or are you just happy to see me?" she asked in her best Groucho Marx voice.

"I'm always happy to see you." He kissed her deeply. "Consider this your engagement present." He pulled out the busk, handing it to her. "They say home is where the heart is. You are my heart. I think I'm home."

She stared at the whalebone. The words united them. "And you expect me to wear it in my corset?"

"Over your heart," he smiled.

"Forever and ever," she responded, smiling back.

* * *

"That was lovely." Marum drifted upward, relief showing in her face.

"It was a good idea to include Georgia. Your handling was nothing short of brilliant."

"We work well together, Sten. You really are a great teacher."

Sten lowered his head, accepting the compliment. "I have news," he told her gravely.

Marum's hand crept to her throat.

"Really, it's nothing terrible, Marum. You've been promoted."

"What?"

"Yes," Sten said, opening his white wings wide. Stretching them to their full extension, he flapped them, rising. "You've been named a guardian. Congratulations."

"I don't know what to say." Marum was shocked by the great honor. "I...like being with you," she added softly.

"I will always be with you," she heard him say as he vanished upward. "Go, Marum. Georgia is waiting to hear from you."

Marum looked at the endless horizon, the sun on one side of the lapis-colored sea, the moon on the other. Boundless stars covered the heavens, and Marum smiled with happiness. Life was good.

The End

AUTHOR'S NOTE

I hope you enjoyed reading *The After House* as much as I enjoyed writing it. The town of Cold Spring Harbor was indeed an important whaling town, where the Jones brothers did run a successful fleet of ships. It became a sort of boomtown as the whaling trade took off. There is no record of a cholera outbreak on Long Island, but Manhattan suffered a major epidemic due to the incoming immigrants and the city's inability to keep up with rapid urban growth.

Hugh, Remy, Captain Eli, and, of course, Georgia and the rest of my characters are all figments of my imagination. While there is a Spring Street in Cold Spring Harbor, the house described in the book does not exist. The church described is loosely based on the church right in town, and it is now a museum. The whaling museum provided not only a wealth of information but also a charming afternoon for my family.

According to the Merriam-Webster Dictionary, the term afterhouse is used as one word to describe a haven on the stern of the ship for sailors to escape the elements. The After House became two words as their story continued on land.

There is a legend of a sperm whale that attacked a whaler, taking all hands down, sometime in the nineteenth century. They say Herman Melville used it as the inspiration for *Moby Dick*.

Made in the USA
Middletown, DE
30 April 2016